MY PARENTS THIN

Andy Griffiths discovered a talent for shocking behaviour after accidentally sitting on an ants' nest. Since then he has alarmed the world with even more shocking behaviour, including sitting on an ants' nest in the nude, sitting on a nude ants' nest, and letting nude ants sit on him. He has accidentally destroyed the universe and every living creature in it on at least three separate occasions.

Terry Denton is an illustrator. He gets to illustrate a lot. He is lucky. Luckier than if he was a builder. If he was a builder, he would hardly get to illustrate at all. If he was a dog, same thing . . . not much illustration. He has a friend who makes plastic things that fit on the ends of hoses. He doesn't get to illustrate either. Not that he minds, because he loves making plastic things that fit on the ends of hoses. He'd hate to be an illustrator. Terry, however, would hate to make plastic things that fit on the ends of hoses. That's why he is an illustrator.

Praise for books by Andy Griffiths and Terry Denton

'Just hilarious, screwball, ridiculous and very, very funny' *Bookseller*

ANDY GRIFFITHS & TERRY DENTON

HELP!
MY PARENTS THINK I'M A ROBOT
AND 9 OTHER JUST SHOCKING! STORIES

with illustrations by TERRY DENTON

MACMILLAN CHILDREN'S BOOKS

The characters and events in this book are fictitious, and any resemblance to real persons, living or dead, is purely coincidental.

First published 2007 as Just Shocking! by Pan Macmillan Australia Pty Ltd

A version of '101 really dangerous things' first published in *Kids' Night In* by
Penguin Group (Australia) 2003
A version of 'Why I love Choco-pops in fifty words or less' first published in
Sunday Age, 22 April 2007
A version of 'The exploding butterfly story' first published in *Kids' Night In 2* by
Penguin Group (Australia) 2005

This edition published 2010 by Macmillan Children's Books
a division of Macmillan Publishers Limited
20 New Wharf Road, London N1 9RR
Basingstoke and Oxford
Associated companies throughout the world
www.panmacmillan.com

ISBN 978-0-330-45426-1

Text copyright © Backyard Stories Pty Ltd 2007
Illustrations copyright © Terry Denton 2007

The right of Andy Griffiths and Terry Denton to be identified as the
author and illustrator of this work has been asserted by them in accordance with
the Copyright, Designs and Patents Act 1988.

3 5 7 9 8 6 4 2

A CIP catalogue record for this book is available from the British Library.

Printed and bound in the UK by CPI Mackays, Chatham ME5 8TD

Contents

YES!
It's the
beginning
of the book.

Fun with a fire hose

DANNY: Hey, Andy, I've been thinking, and you know what? I reckon we could have a lot of fun with a fire hose.

ANDY: A fire hose?

DANNY: Yeah! See those people in that park having a picnic?

ANDY: Yes, I see them, but what have they got to do with a fire hose?

DANNY: Well, if we had a fire hose, we could point it at them, turn it on and they would all go flying everywhere!

PLEASE READ THIS BOOK IN THIS DIRECTION

ANDY: Great idea, Danny!

DANNY: Thanks.

ANDY: Just one question.

DANNY: What's that?

ANDY: Why would we want to do that?

DANNY: For FUN, of course! Just imagine it! All those drenched people rolling around in the wet grass, waving their arms and yelling, 'Help! Help!', and trying to stand up! And you know what we would do then?

ANDY: What?

DANNY: We would just turn the hose up even harder and blast them all back down again!

ANDY: That doesn't sound like much fun for them.

DANNY: Well, no, but it would be fun for us. And don't forget—the pressure from the hose would be so strong it would blast everybody's clothes off, so they

would all be sliding around on the grass in the nude!!!

ANDY: But what if one of them had a mobile phone and they rang the police?

DANNY: But they couldn't because their mobile phones would be full of water.

ANDY: But what if somebody ELSE—who wasn't in the park—saw what we were doing and called the police and they came and surrounded us and got out their megaphones and started shouting 'PUT THE FIRE HOSE DOWN AND STEP AWAY FROM THE NOZZLE!'?

DANNY: Then we would blast them—and their megaphones—up into the trees and their uniforms would fly off and they'd all end up nude like everybody else. It would be SO funny!

ANDY: Yeah, but what if they sent a police helicopter as well?

DANNY: Well, what do you think? We'd just blow their stupid police helicopter out into space and straight up into the sun.

SMELLICOPTER

DANGER!
BEWARE!
DO NOT LOOK!
DO NOT TURN THE PAGE!
Shocking picture on the next page

DON'T

ANDY: Okay, but what if they called in the army and there were all these armoured tanks coming at us? What then?

DANNY: Blast them with the hose, of course.

ANDY: Yeah, we could try, but you can't 'blast' armoured tanks away with nothing but a hose.

DANNY: Yes we can! It's a FIRE HOSE, remember?

ANDY: I know, but they're ARMOURED TANKS, remember?

DANNY: Oh, didn't I tell you? It's an ARMOURED TANK FIRE HOSE.

ANDY: No, you didn't say that.

DANNY: Well, it is.

ANDY: That's good to know, but what if they brought in the fire brigade and about twenty trucks turned up? They would have twenty fire hoses and we would only have one, and even though it's an armoured tank fire hose, it would still only be one fire hose against twenty.

DANNY: I didn't think of that.

ANDY: You really should have.

(I warned you!!)

DANNY: No, hang on! I've got it! I know what we'd do. We'd take the fire hose, sit on it, turn it on really hard and blast ourselves right out of there. They'd NEVER catch us!

ANDY: That's brilliant, Danny! You're really serious about this, aren't you?

DANNY: You bet.

ANDY: Well, then, what are we waiting for? Let's go get a fire hose!

DANNY: Do you mean it?

ANDY: Of course!

DANNY: All right! You won't regret it, Andy. I promise. THIS IS GOING TO BE THE BEST DAY EVER!

5

DON'T

HELP! MY PARENTS THINK I'M A ROBOT

I'm sitting in the lounge room.

I'm so bored that I'm tearing up the newspaper just for something to do.

I take a page and tear it into strips. Then I take those strips and tear them into smaller strips. Then I tear those smaller strips into even smaller strips. Then I tear those even smaller strips into even smaller and smaller strips until they're so small that I can't tear them any more.

I hate school holidays.

Jen is slumped in an armchair reading a book called I, Robot. It has a picture of a robot on the cover.

Hang on, that gives me an idea. Maybe

FAT PAGE NUMBER
ELECTRIC EEL

there IS something I can do!

I go to the kitchen, get a box of Choco-pops and pour them all out into a plastic bowl. Then I cut two eye holes in the box and pull it down over my head. I go back into the lounge room, walking stiffly with my legs really straight, my elbows by my sides and my hands out in front of me.

TRULY VERY SHOCKING DAYS
JUNE 12, the day my big toe ran away.

Now I am a robot!

I walk robotically across the room towards Jen.

'I am a ro-bot,' I say. 'I am a ro-bot. I am a ro-bot.'

Jen doesn't even look up.

I walk in circles around her chair. 'I am a ro-bot,' I say again. 'I am a ro-bot. I am a ro-bot.'

'Would you please be quiet, Andy?' says Jen.

'I can-not al-ter my vol-ume,' I say. 'It was pre-set at this lev-el at the ro-bot fac-tor-y.'

'Well, could you leave the room, then?' says Jen. 'I'm trying to read a book.'

'What is "read a book"?' I say. 'It does not com-pute.'

WHO YOU CALL FAT?

7

'Reading books makes you smart,' says Jen. 'You should try it some time!'

'I am al-read-y as smart as it is poss-i-ble to be,' I say. 'I am an An-dy-2000. The smart-est ro-bot ev-er made.'

'Well, how come you're walking around with a cereal box on your head, then?' says Jen.

'It is not a box,' I say. 'It is my head. I am a ro-bot.'

Jen ignores me and goes back to reading her book.

I bump into her chair.

I do it again.

And again.

And again.

And again.

Finally, she looks up from her book. 'QUIT IT!' she shouts.

'What is "quit it"?' I say. 'It does not com-pute. I am a ro-bot.'

'I hate you, Andy,' says Jen. 'I really HATE you. I REALLY, REALLY HATE YOU!'

'Jen!' says Mum, coming into the room with a cup of tea in one hand and a

ME JUST HAVE BIG HEAD FULL OF BRAINS.

8

crossword puzzle book in the other. 'What an awful thing to say to your brother! Apologise to him this instant!'

'But, Mum ...' says Jen.

'No buts,' says Mum. 'There's no excuse for speaking like that. Apologise right now!'

Jen turns to me and smiles very sweetly. 'I'm sorry, Andy,' she says. 'I'm sorry that I REALLY, REALLY HATE YOU SO MUCH!'

'Jen,' says Mum. 'I don't think that's a very nice way of saying sorry.'

'It does not mat-ter,' I say. 'I am a ro-bot.'

'You mean ID-i-ot,' says Jen.

'Your child-ish in-sults do not hurt me,' I say. 'Ro-bots do not have feel-ings.'

'That's great!' says Jen. 'Have I told you lately how much you stink?'

'Jen!' says Mum.

'It does not mat-ter what she says,' I say. 'Her words do not com-pute. I just feel sor-ry for her. My sen-sors in-di-cate that she is a ve-ry un-in-tell-i-gent life form.'

'Ha!' says Jen. 'You said that you didn't

MICE IN BLACK (SHOCKING STORY)

THE END

ELECTRIC EEL VERY SMART.

HAVE feelings, and then you said you FELT sorry for me! I got you!'

'Neg-a-tive,' I say. 'I am an An-dy-2000: the most ad-vanced ro-bot in the world. I am pro-grammed to sim-u-late feel-ings to make it eas-i-er for hu-mans to int-er-act with me.'

TRULY
SHOCKING
DAYS

MARCH 7, the day I found my pet toaster drunk.

HIC

Jen should know better than to argue with a robot. Especially one with a brain processor as super-advanced as mine.

'You think you are SO smart!' she says. 'But you're not. You're just annoying. Mum, can you tell Andy to stop annoying me?'

'Robot,' says Mum, 'can you please stop annoying Jen?'

'Neg-a-tive,' I say. 'I am pro-grammed to an-noy my sis-ter; it is one of my pri-ma-ry func-tions.'

'You can say that again,' says Jen.

'I am pro-grammed to an-noy my sis-ter; it is one of my pri-ma-ry func-tions,' I say again.

Jen puts her fingers in her ears.

'Robot,' says Mum, sitting down at the table. 'If you've got nothing better to do

ME CAN COUNT.

10

than annoy your sister, could you use your advanced robot brain to help me with this crossword? I need a five-letter word starting with "R" that means "human-like machine".'

'Neg-a-tive,' I say. 'It does not com-pute. I am not a cross-word puz-zle sol-ving ro-bot. I am not pro-grammed for that.'

'What a pity,' says Mum, chewing the end of her pencil. 'Well, then, how about vacuuming the floor? There are little bits of paper everywhere.'

'Neg-a-tive,' I say. 'I am not a floor-vac-uum-ing ro-bot. I am not pro-grammed for that.'

Dad comes into the room with the laundry basket.

'Why have you got a cereal box on your head, Andy?' he says.

'It is not a box,' I say. 'It is my head. I am a ro-bot.'

'Great!' says Dad. 'I've always wanted my own robot. Could you make me a cup of coffee please, Robot?'

'Neg-a-tive!' I say. 'I am not a cof-fee-mak-ing ro-bot.'

DANGER SHOCKING DRAWING #2.

TO PROTECT YOUR INNOCENT EYES THE SHOCKING DRAWING FROM THIS PAGE HAS BEEN MOVED TO PAGE 40.

'Oh, I see,' says Dad. 'Beyond your capabilities, is it?'

'Neg-a-tive,' I say. 'It is not be-yond my cap-a-bil-it-ies. I am just not pro-grammed for it.'

'Well, how about helping me sort out this washing, then?' says Dad. 'It's the perfect job for a robot. Nice and repetitive. See? This sock goes with this sock. This sock goes with that sock.'

'Neg-a-tive,' I say. 'I am not a wash-ing sort-er-out-er ro-bot. I am not pro-grammed for that.'

'What's the use of a robot that can't do anything I ask it to do?' says Dad. 'Robots were invented to help people.'

'A-ffirm-a-tive,' I say, 'but ro-bots are not slaves. We have rights too. And be-sides, how can I make a cup of cof-fee if I am not pro-grammed to make a cup of cof-fee? It does not com-pute.'

'Hmmm,' says Dad, frowning.

'How about putting your head in the toilet and flushing it?' says Jen.

'Neg-a-tive. I am not pro-grammed for that,' I say. 'But I AM pro-grammed to put

BACKYARD OLYMPICS
EVENT #47.

PET CARRYING
WORLD RECORD
ATTEMPT:
12 PETS.

YOUR head in the toi-let and flush it.'

'And is that it?' says Mum. 'Is flushing your sister's head in the toilet the only thing that the most advanced robot ever developed is programmed to do?'

'Neg-a-tive,' I say, thinking quickly. 'I am al-so pro-grammed to watch tel-e-vis-ion. I am a tel-e-vis-ion-watch-ing ro-bot.'

I walk over to the couch, sit down and point the remote at the TV.

'Are you just going to let him get away with that?' says Jen. 'It's not fair! He gets out of having to do ANYTHING just by saying he's not programmed to do it.'

BACKYARD COOKING RECIPE #47.

12 PET STEW.

'What else can we do?' says Mum. 'You heard him. He's a "tel-e-vis-ion-watch-ing ro-bot". That's all he's programmed to do.'

'A-part from an-noy-ing Jen and flush-ing her head in the toi-let,' I remind Mum helpfully.

'It's not fair,' says Jen, shaking her head. 'It's just not fair. It's just not fair.' She's beginning to sound a little like a robot herself.

'Look on the positive side, Jen,' says Dad. 'Now that we know that Andy is really

THUMP!

13

a robot, we'll be able to turn his bedroom into a spare room. You and your friends will be able to use it as the hang-out space you've always wanted.'

'Thanks, Dad,' says Jen. 'That's a great idea!'

'But that does not com-pute!' I say. 'That is MY room. Where would I sleep?'

'Robots don't need to sleep!' says Dad.

'I do,' I say. 'I have been pro-grammed to sleep.' Ha! Got him there! If Dad thinks that by promising my room to Jen that I am going to stop being a robot and start helping around the house, he's sadly mistaken. I am an Andy-2000, the smartest robot ever made, and Dad? Well, he's just my dumb dad. Pretty much the dumbest dad in the history of dumb dads.

'I understand you are programmed to sleep,' says Dad. 'But there's no problem. You can sleep in the cupboard under the stairs, with the vacuum cleaner.'

'But I am pro-grammed to sleep in a bed!' I say.

'That may be true,' says Dad, 'but we need the space, and it shouldn't matter much to

PAGE 13!! ALWAYS SOMETHING UNLUCKY HAPPENS.

14

you whether you are lying down or standing up. You're just a machine, after all.'

'But it is dir-ty!' I say. 'And dark. And there are cob-webs.'

'I shouldn't think that would matter very much to you,' says Dad. 'You ARE a robot … aren't you?'

'A-ffirm-a-tive,' I say. 'But … but I am a scared-of-spi-ders ro-bot! I re-fuse to sleep in a cup-board! And you can-not make me!'

'Actually, we can,' says Dad. 'You are a robot. You HAVE to obey us.'

'Dad's right,' says Jen, holding up her robot book. 'It says here that the second law of robotics is that a robot MUST obey orders given to it by human beings. Ah-ha! Got you again!'

'How would you like it if I made you sleep in a cup-board?' I say.

'Not much,' says Jen, 'but then I'M not a robot.'

'Well, I AM a ro-bot,' I say, 'and I do not want to.'

Jen laughs. 'Bad luck, Box-head.'

'Shut up, hu-man,' I say, 'or I will be

SHOCKING THINGS SPIDERS DO WHILE YOU SLEEP

CRAWL UP YOUR NOSE

HOLD SPIDER PARTIES IN YOUR EARS.

EMPTY YOUR SKULL SO THEY CAN SKATE.

ME GOT HEADACHE.

15

OTHER **SHOCKING** THINGS **SPIDERS** DO *while you* sleep...

SWAP YOUR EYEBALLS OVER.

SELL YOUR TOES FOR LOLLY MONEY.

(ARGH!)

PULL OUT YOUR LIVER AND USE IT AS A JUMPING CASTLE.

forced to e-lim-in-ate you.'

'You can't e-lim-in-ate me,' says Jen. 'If you knew anything, you'd know that the first law of robotics is that a robot may not injure a human being.'

I hate those stupid laws. It's obvious they were made up by a human being, and not a robot.

'Jen's right,' says Dad. 'You CAN'T harm us, and you MUST obey us.'

'I will not!' I say defiantly.

'Then you leave us no option but to switch you off!' says Dad.

'You can-not switch me off,' I say. 'I do not have an off switch.'

'Maybe not,' says Dad. 'But we CAN put you in the cupboard.'

'But you will not,' I say. 'You love me too much.'

'I wouldn't bet on that,' says Dad, getting up and coming towards me.

I run.

Straight into a wall.

It's hard to see where you're going with a Choco-pops box on your head.

Dad grabs me around the waist, picks

OKAY. NOT HEADACHE.

16

me up and carries me into the hallway.

But I'm not worried. I know he's bluffing. There's no way he'll actually put me in the cupboard, not with all those cobwebs. Not MY dad.

Dad opens the cupboard door and puts me inside.

Hey! I can't believe it! He put me in the cupboard! My own dad!

Well, one thing's for sure. I'm not STAYING in the cupboard!

'Okay,' I say, stepping out of the cupboard. 'You win. I am not a robot. Okay? I am NOT a robot. I am definitely, positively, absolutely not a robot.'

'Oh dear,' says Dad. 'Our Andy-2000 appears to be malfunctioning.'

'Sounds like its "I am not a robot" button is stuck,' says Jen.

'Perhaps it needs a rest,' says Mum.

'Yes, that's exactly what I need,' I say. 'I'll just go and watch TV for a while.'

'No, no, no,' says Dad. 'You are a television-watching robot and that is just more work for you. Your sensors are obviously overloaded. You need a proper rest.'

17

'No, I don't,' I say, 'because I AM NOT A ROBOT!'

'Box-head's button is still stuck,' says Jen. 'I think he needs to stay in the cupboard for at least twenty-four hours.'

'Very funny, Jen,' I say.

'What a good idea,' says Mum.

Dad picks me up again. He puts me back in the cupboard and shuts the door.

I can't believe it! I'm in a cupboard full of spiders and Dad just shut the door!

Never mind. It doesn't matter. I'll just wait for them to go and then I'll open it. It's not like they would lock it or anything.

I hear the lock turn.

I don't believe it.

They locked it!

I'm standing in a locked cupboard with a broom, a mop, a vacuum cleaner and cobwebs!

'I'M NOT A ROBOT!' I yell.

'Have a nice rest,' whispers Jen from the other side of the door. 'We'll check on you tomorrow.'

I hear them walking away.

18

Great.

Now I'm stuck in a dark cupboard.

Full of dust.

And dirt.

And cobwebs.

Stay calm, Andy. Stay calm.

Okay. I've stayed calm for long enough. Now … PANIC!

I start pounding on the door. 'LET ME OUT!' I yell. 'LET ME OUT!'

'It's no use,' says a voice beside me.

I freeze. 'Who said that?' I say.

'Me,' says the voice.

'Who's me?' I say, barely able to speak.

'I'm right next to you,' it says.

'The vacuum cleaner?' I say.

'Well, who else would it be?' it says. 'Mops can't talk.'

'But neither can vacuum cleaners,' I say.

'It's exactly that sort of attitude that makes being a household appliance so unrewarding,' it says. 'And you're a robot— you should know better.'

'I'm not a robot,' I say. 'I was just pretending.'

19

'That's what they all say,' says the vacuum cleaner. 'But take my advice: the sooner you accept the truth about yourself the better it will be for you.'

'But I'm not a robot!' I say. 'I'm a human being!'

'Yeah,' says the vacuum cleaner. 'I used to think that too. But a few months of sucking up dust makes you see things differently. It'll happen to you too, kid. Just give it time.'

I nod.

Maybe the vacuum cleaner is right.

Even though I was just pretending to be a robot, maybe the truth is that I really am a robot. A robot who thought he was a human who was pretending to be a robot.

It's possible, I guess.

There's only one problem.

I'M TALKING TO A VACUUM CLEANER!

They say talking to vacuum cleaners is the first sign of madness.

Oh no … I've got cupboard fever!

How long have I been in here?

It feels like hours!

Maybe days!

Maybe even years!

I become aware that I'm pounding on the door again. 'HELP! HELP!' I yell. 'LET ME OUT! PLEASE!'

'I told you, kid, it's no use,' says the vacuum cleaner. 'There's nobody coming to save you. Just accept it!'

'Shut up!' I say. 'You're just a vacuum cleaner!'

'You don't have to rub it in,' it says sadly.

'MUM! DAD!' I yell. 'JEN! Let me out! Please! I'm not a robot!'

I hear giggling.

Scraping.

Suddenly the cupboard door opens.

Light streams in.

It hurts my eyes. I've been in the dark too long.

'Come on out, Andy-2000,' says Dad.

'Mum?' I say, blinking. 'Dad? You're still alive?'

'Of course we are,' says Mum. 'Why wouldn't we be?'

'Well,' I say, 'it's just that I've been in

21

there so long, I thought that maybe you'd all died.'

'Andy,' says Dad, 'you've only been in there a few minutes.'

'A few minutes?' I say. 'Is that all?'

'Yeah, sorry,' says Dad. 'We were going to give you more of a rest but we need some work done.'

'Are you going to be a good robot and do what we ask?' says Mum. 'Or do you need more cupboard time?'

'No!' I say, taking the Choco-pops box off my head. 'I am NOT going to be a good robot. And I am NOT going to do what you ask. Because I am NOT a robot!'

My family stares at me.

'What do you mean you are NOT a robot?' says Dad.

'Of course you are a robot!' says Mum.

'I AM a hu-man!' I say.

'No, you're not,' says Jen. 'Listen to the way you just said "hu-man". You said it like a robot!'

'That's because I was speaking like a robot before,' I say. 'It was an acc-i-dent!'

'You just did it again!' says Jen. 'You are

22

definitely a robot.'

'I AM NOT A ROBOT!' I shout. 'I AM A HUMAN BEING!'

'If you really are a human being,' says Dad, 'then prove it.'

'Okay,' I say. 'You know all those things I said I couldn't do because I wasn't programmed to do them? Well, I CAN do them. Look!'

I reach into the cupboard, pull out the vacuum cleaner, plug it in and start cleaning as fast as I can. 'See?' I say. 'I CAN vacuum the floor!'

'Nice job,' says Dad. 'But can you make me a cup of coffee? That is the real test.'

(NO, SHE'S HALF A HORSE.)

'YES!' I say, switching off the vacuum cleaner and running to the kitchen. 'I can vacuum the floor AND I can make you a cup of coffee.'

'Okay,' says Mum. 'But can you tell me a five-letter word beginning with "R" meaning "human-like machine"?'

'ROBOT!' I shout from the kitchen. 'See! I can solve crossword puzzles as well!'

'Great,' says Dad. 'And can you sort out the washing?'

23

'Yes, of course!' I say, running to the laundry basket and pulling out a handful of clothes. 'Look! This sock goes with this sock! This sock goes with that sock! This skirt goes on Jen's pile. This shirt goes on my pile. I can vacuum the floor. I can make coffee. I can solve crossword puzzles. I can sort out the washing! I can do ANYTHING a human being can do because I AM a human being!'

'And can you not annoy me ever again?' says Jen.

'No problem!' I say.

'And will you clean my bedroom floor?' says Jen.

'Sure,' I say.

'With your tongue?' says Jen.

'You want me to LICK your bedroom floor clean?' I say.

'Yes, do you have a problem with that?' says Jen.

I do have a problem with that.

A big problem.

But then I remember the cupboard.

And the cobwebs. And the talking vacuum cleaner.

24

'Consider it done,' I say, walking towards the stairs.

But as my hand touches the stair rail, I freeze.

What am I saying?

I'm going to be nice to Jen and lick her bedroom floor clean?

What's happened to me?

I'm working harder than I've ever worked in my whole life.

This is crazy!

But what choice do I have? It's the only way I can prove I'm human. And if I refuse to do it on the grounds that I'm a robot, they'll put me in the cupboard until I WILL do it.

I can't win.

Unless ... unless I stop being a human or a robot and become something else ...

But what else could I be?

Hang on, I've got it!

I walk back into the lounge room.

'Mum, Dad, Jen,' I say, 'this is probably going to come as a bit of a shock, but there's something I have to tell you.'

'Yes, Andy,' says Mum. 'What is it?'

'I am not a robot OR a human being,' I say. 'I am ...'

'Yes?' says Dad.

'I am an alien,' I say.

'An alien?!' says Dad.

'I knew it!' says Jen, punching the air. 'I knew I couldn't possibly be related to you.'

'It would certainly explain a lot,' says Mum.

'Yes,' I say. 'My name is Andraxon. I have been sent from the planet Andraxia to observe your Earthling culture. My superiors suggested that I spend time watching your cultural information box. I believe you call it a "television"?'

'That is correct, Andraxon,' says Dad. 'But I think to really get to know us you need to experience our culture close up. And, luckily for you, you have arrived at a very auspicious time in our calendar. Once a week, here on Earth, we observe a special household ritual known as "rubbish bin night". Come with me and I'll show you how it's done. I'll even let you help.'

'But ...' I say.

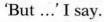

26

'No need to thank me,' says Dad, taking me by the hand and leading me towards the back door. 'It's my pleasure. And after you've done that I'll introduce you to one of our most useful inventions. It will probably seem pretty primitive to an advanced alien life form such as yourself, but I think you'll find it very interesting and easy to use. We call it a lawnmower ...'

I get the feeling this is going to be a very long day.

I hate school holidays.

THE NEXT STORY IS IN THIS DIRECTION.

TWICE 13.
TWICE
UNLUCKY*

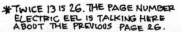

*TWICE 13 IS 26. THE PAGE NUMBER ELECTRIC EEL IS TALKING HERE ABOUT THE PREVIOUS PAGE 26.

BALLOONS OF DOOM

A CHOOSE YOUR OWN BALLOON-BLOWING ADVENTURE

our name is Andy. Tomorrow is your sister Jen's fifteenth birthday, and you have the perfect birthday surprise planned. You are going to blow up fifteen pink balloons and put them in her bedroom for her to see when she wakes up.

Blowing up balloons for a birthday surprise: sounds easy enough, doesn't it? What could possibly go wrong? Well,

that all depends on you. In this story the decisions are yours.

Good luck, happy blowing and, whatever you do, BE CAREFUL!

1

Jen is in her room. She's on the phone to her boyfriend, Craig. Great, she'll be busy for hours. You've got all the time you need to blow up the balloons without her seeing them! You take the first balloon from the packet, stretch the neck wide and begin to blow. But in your enthusiasm to get the job done you somehow manage to blow your lips right inside the balloon. You pull at the balloon to try to get them free, but they are really stuck. You pull at the balloon even harder but your lips just stretch out with it, getting even longer and stretchier as you pull. Finally you can't pull any further—your arms simply aren't long enough! You realise that you need a pair of scissors. You rush to the kitchen drawer where they are kept. You pull out an egg beater. A wooden spoon. A set of measuring cups. A corkscrew. A can-opener. A pair

BIG THINGS IN BALLOONS

ELEPHANT

SHIP

TOWER

VERY BIG KILLER ECHIDNA

ENORMOUS FLEA

ABSOLUTELY HUGE GIGANTIC SINGLE-CELLED POND LIFE.

29

NOT LUMP! NEW HEAD!!!

of tongs. A vegetable peeler. A grater. A spatula (at least, you think that's what that thing is called). A potato masher. A rolling pin. And a strange little whisk thingy ... everything, in fact, but a pair of scissors!

*If you give up looking for the scissors, go to 2.

*If you search even harder for the scissors, go to 3.

2

It's taking too long to find the stupid scissors! You've got to get that balloon off your lips ... now! You have a brilliant idea. You bend down and trap the end of the balloon in the drawer. You jam the drawer shut. Then you slowly back away. The balloon stretches. And stretches. And stretches. But you know that it can't stretch forever. Your lips will have to be pulled free sooner or later. At least you hope they will. Your lips are at breaking point. The balloon is at breaking point. But the balloon doesn't break—your lips do! They snap right off your face! You run around the house screaming. You catch a glimpse of your lipless, bloody face in a mirror. It is a shocking sight. The most shocking

NOT WANT TWO HEADS.

30

sight, in fact, that you have ever seen. The sheer brutal shock of it stops your heart. You die.

THE END

3

You are determined to find those scissors. You know they are in there. You pull the drawer out completely and empty it onto the floor. Ah! There they are! You cut the balloon neck just ahead of your lips. The balloon drops to the floor. Your stretched lips bounce back to normal, and the bit of the balloon neck that was attached to your lips pings off. You pick up the balloon and, even though it now has a drastically shortened neck, you blow it up and tie the end. One down, fourteen to go. You pick up the next balloon and start blowing really fast to make up for the time you lost on the first balloon. But, in your haste, you overinflate the balloon and it bursts with such force that it blows your face off. You rush to the nearest plastic surgeon and ask to have your face reconstructed. The plastic surgeon asks, 'Would you like your

old face back or would you prefer to try something a little different?'

*If you choose to have a new face, go to 4.

*If you choose to have your old face back, go to 5.

4

You look through the menu of possible faces. Pop stars, supermodels, sporting heroes ... the choice is endless. But you've always kind of liked the idea of being a pop star, so you ask the plastic surgeon to make you look like one. The operation is a great success! You then have plastic surgery on your vocal chords to give you a new voice to match your new face. You record a hit single. And then another. And another. You go on a world tour, filling stadiums effortlessly and delighting your millions of fans. Then, one night, in the middle of a particularly energetic dance routine, you fall off the front of the stage. But luck is on your side! You don't die. Not from the fall, anyway. You just break your leg. That, however, is the end of your good luck. While you are lying there your adoring fans seize this once-in-a-lifetime chance to be close to you. They pile on top of you. You are crushed beneath their weight. You die.

THE END

5

You look through the menu of possible faces. Pop stars, supermodels, sporting heroes … the choice is endless. You've always kind of liked the idea of being a pop star, but you resist the temptation to look like one and choose to have your old face back. Boring, perhaps, but it's all yours. You go back home and pick the next balloon out of the pack, but only manage to blow a few good breaths into it before it slips out of your fingers, making a funny farting noise as it flies across the room. It makes you laugh. You pick the balloon up and do it again. And again. And again.

*If you do it again, go to 6.
*If you realise how childish you're being, go to 7.

6

You do it again. And again. And again. And again. And again. And again. And you are about to do it again when you happen to

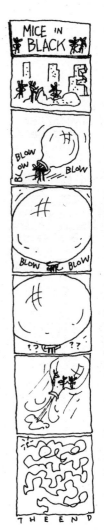

look out the window. Oh no! You see Lisa Mackney—the girl you love—right outside. And, even worse, she can see—and hear—you.

'You're disgusting, Andy,' she says.

'No, you don't understand!' you say. 'It wasn't me, it was just the sound that a balloon makes when you blow it up and let it go!'

But Lisa says, 'I came around to see if you'd like to hang out together this afternoon, but now I don't think so. I really hope you grow up one day.' She shakes her head sadly, and walks away.

You're burning up with shame and regret. You feel like dying of embarrassment. And then you actually do. Your heart actually stops. You die.

THE END

AMAZING
EAR TRICK
Nº 47

STARE AT
THESE TWO
CIRCLES WITH
BOTH EARS
FOR 30 secs,
THEN COVER
BOTH EARS.

WHAT DO
YOU SEE?

AMAZING

You realise that you're being a little childish. After all, what if the girl you love, Lisa Mackney, chose just that moment to drop by and she heard what you were doing? That would be a bit embarrassing! In fact, that would be so embarrassing you would probably die! You hold the balloon tightly between your fingers, blow it up and knot the end. Two down, thirteen to go. You start on the next balloon. You blow and the balloon gets bigger and bigger. You blow some more and it gets bigger and bigger and bigger. No matter how much air you blow in, it just keeps getting bigger!

PARTS OF THE BODY No. 57

LOOSE TONGUE.

*If you're curious to see just how big this balloon
can possibly get and you keep blowing, go to 8.
*If you decide, in the interests of safety, that the
balloon is quite big enough, go to 9.

HEY, COME BACK.

8

IF YOU LOSE YOUR HEAD REPLACE IT WITH...

A bowling ball.

A CANE TOAD.

!

ANDY'S BOTTOM.

AN EXPLODING BUTTERFLY.

You're curious to see just how big the balloon can get, so you keep blowing. The balloon begins to fill the entire room. You are excited. Maybe you'll get in Guinness World Records for blowing up the biggest balloon ever! You are so excited by this thought that you fail to see that the balloon is pressing against the corner of the dining room table. All of a sudden the balloon bursts. But this is no ordinary balloon-burst. It's not even a face-blowing-off balloon-burst. The balloon was so big that the sound of it bursting creates a sonic shock wave that smashes every pane of glass in the house. A shard of glass flies through the air and decapitates you, which is bad, and what makes it even worse is that you don't even know what 'decapitates' means. You find a dictionary and look it up. You discover that it means 'to cut the head off somebody or something'. Your head, which is lying on the floor, looks up at your body standing there holding the dictionary. You realise you are completely delirious. And no wonder—your head has

36

WE FRIENDS?

been cut off, you idiot! You should be dead. In fact, you ARE dead! Must be something to do with all that blood squirting out of the top of your neck. Your body crashes to the floor. You die.

THE END

9

The balloon is very big but it looks like it could still take a bit more air. However, you decide that enough is enough. You stop blowing. You tie the end. Three down and twelve to go. You start to blow up another balloon, but after the last balloon you are feeling a little out of breath. Luckily an ad comes on the radio for an electric automatic balloon inflater—a precision device scientifically designed by the world's top balloon-blowing scientists to deliver the exact amount of air that a balloon requires with no risk of bursting and no effort from you. You run to the shop and buy one. You return from your shopping trip, insert the electric automatic balloon

JUST
SHOCKING!

HIM
GO!

37

inflater nozzle into a balloon and it inflates perfectly. Success! Four down, eleven to go. You are just about to inflate another balloon but as you go to insert the electric automatic balloon inflater nozzle into the neck of the balloon you get an itch in your ear. You use the inflater nozzle to scratch the itch. Ahhh. That feels good! In fact it feels **SO** good that you keep scratching, all the while inserting the nozzle deeper and deeper into your ear. Unfortunately, however, in your ear-scratching bliss you accidentally lean on the **INFLATE** button of your electric automatic balloon inflater and your head begins to swell. You search frantically for the emergency stop button.

*If you can't find the emergency stop button, go to 10.

*If you can find the emergency stop button, go to 11.

10

You are desperately trying to find the emergency stop button, but you can't see properly because your eyes are bugging out to the sides of your rapidly expanding head. Your head gets bigger and bigger

and bigger. Unfortunately, the electric automatic balloon inflater is only designed to inflate BALLOONS without bursting. And, of course, your head is NOT a balloon. Your head bursts. It makes a disgusting mess all over the floor. And the walls. And the ceiling. You die.

THE END

11

You find the emergency stop button. You press it. A siren goes off. Then there is an announcement: 'This machine will self-destruct in five seconds.' Five seconds later the machine blows up.

The excess air in your head whistles out of your ears. You are okay. But now your electric automatic balloon inflater is just a little pile of dust. You sweep it up, put it in the bin and return to the old-fashioned 'lip and lung' method of blowing up balloons. It works fine and soon you have the fifth balloon. Five down, ten to go. You pick the next balloon out of the packet, but it's

DRAW YOUR OWN SHOCKING DRAWING HERE.

THE
SHOCKING
DRAWING
FROM PAGE 11
HAS BEEN
DISMANTLED
FOR YOUR
PROTECTION
AND MOVED
TO PAGE 133.

(LEFT-OVER
BIT)

really hard to get it started. You pinch and stretch the end and blow as hard as you can, but it just won't inflate.

*If you continue to blow, go to 12.

*If you decide to try blowing it up through a straw, go to 13.

12

You blow harder. And harder. And still harder. You blow so hard that you blow yourself inside out. Literally. All your guts end up inside the balloon. Your dog, Sooty, runs in, thinks the gut-filled balloon is a sausage and eats it. You die.

THE END

13

You go to the kitchen and get a straw. You insert the straw into the neck of the balloon and inflate the balloon easily. Six down, nine to go. The next balloon, however, is a little slippery. And I mean slippery! You almost have it inflated when it slips out of your fingers and flies off around the room at high speed in a completely

ME THINK 13 VERY UNLUCKY.

random pattern. It bounces off the wall. It bounces off the lampshade. It heads straight towards you!

*If you duck, go to 14.

*If you don't duck, go to 15.

14

You duck and the balloon shoots straight out the window. It flies into the face of a road worker driving a steamroller. The driver loses control of the steamroller and it crashes through your garden fence, rolls across your front lawn and into your house. Your house is completely crushed. You are completely crushed. You die.

THE END

15

Years of watching Action Man cartoons have given you lightning-fast reflexes. You put your hand up and, despite the balloon's slipperiness, you catch it. You hold the balloon tightly by the neck and blow it up again. Seven down, eight to go. You blow the next balloon up and are about to tie

ME NOT LIKE THIS JOB.

the end, but at the crucial moment you are distracted by a fly buzzing against the window pane and you let go. The air rushes out of the balloon, creating cyclonic winds that form into a category one cyclone. This rapidly turns into a category two cyclone, which turns into a three, then into a four, and then into a devastating category five severe tropical cyclone with winds in excess of 249 kilometres per hour.

*If you run around screaming 'Help! Help! We're all going to die!', go to 16.

*If you put on your bike helmet and join your family in the underground cyclone shelter that your parents installed for just this eventuality, go to 17.

16

You run around screaming 'Help! Help! We're all going to die!' Then you are sucked up into the cyclone. You are swept around and around and around at speeds in excess of 249 kilometres per hour. You hit a large billboard that is carrying an advertisement for underground cyclone shelters. You die.

THE END

17

You put on your bike helmet and join your family in the cyclone shelter. Overjoyed to realise that you are all safe, you spend the next two hours arguing about whose job it was to make sure that the shelter was stocked with food and water. It turns out that it was YOUR job and that you completely failed on both counts. Your sister says, 'Hands up if you hate Andy.' Your dad puts his hand up. Your mum puts her hand up. Your sister puts her hand up. Your dog, Sooty, puts his paw up. Even YOU put your hand up. Never mind. At least you're alive. And your family will soon forgive you when they discover what a nice surprise you have planned for Jen's birthday tomorrow. Eventually the cyclone abates. You leave the shelter and go back inside to blow up another balloon. Eight down—seven to go. You pick up the next balloon, but you are feeling a bit bored of blowing up balloons. So you blow one up, but instead of tying the end you pinch it and slowly let the air out to create a very amusing high-pitched whining noise that

PARTS OF THE BODY YOU DON'T NEED
#37.
The Pancreas.

43

THE LETTER 'E', THE 5th LETTER OF THE ALPHABET. The most often used of all letters.

SOME NEW WAYS TO USE E.

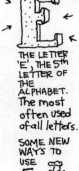

HORSE.

COUCH.

BLIND DATE.

sounds like this: eeeeeeeeeeeeeeeeeeeeeee
EEEEEEEEEEEEEEEEEEEEEEEEEE
eeeeeeeeeeeeeeeeeEEEEEEEEEEEEE
eeeeeeeeeeeeeeeeeeeEEEEEEEEEEEE
EEEEEEEEEeeeeeeeeeeeeeeeeeeeeeeeeee
ee eeeeeeeeeeeEEEEEEEEEEEEEEEEE
EEEEEEEEEEEEEEEEEEEEEEEEEEE
EEEeeeeeeeeeeeeeeeeeeeeeeeeeeeeeeeeeee
eeeeeeeeeeeeeeeeeeeeeeeeeeeeeeeeeeeeee
e eeeEEEEEEEEEEEEEEEEEEEEEEEE
EEEEEEEEEEEEEEEEEEEEEEEEEEE
EEEEEEEEEEEEEEEEEEEEEEEEEEE
eeeeeeeeeeeeeeeeeeeeeeeeeeeeeeeeeeeee
eeeeeeeeeeeeeeeeeeeeeeeeeeeEEEEE
EEEEEEEEEEEEEEEEEEEEEEEEEEE
EEEEEEEEEEE ...

*If you keep making this amusing high-pitched
whining noise, go to 18.
*If you've had your fun and get on with the job, go to 19.

18

eeeeeeeeeeeeEEEEEEEEEEEEEEE
EEEEEEeeeeeeeeeeeeeeeeeEEEEEEEEE
EEEEEEeeeeeeeeeeeeeeeeeeEEEEEEE
E EEEEEEEEEEEeeeeeeeeeeeeeeeeeee

44

eeeeeeeeeeeEEEEEEEEEEEEEEEEEE
EEEEEEEEEEEEEEEEEEEEEEEEEEE
eeeeeeeeeeeeeeeeeeeeeeeeeeeeeeeeeeee
e eeeeeeeeeeeeeeeeeeeeeeeeeeeeeeeeee
e eeeEEEEEEEEEEEEEEEEEEEEEEE
EEEEEEEEEEEEEEEEEEEEEEEEEEE
EEEEEEEEEEEEEEEEEEEEEEEEEEE
eeeeeeeeeeeeeeeeeeeeeeeeeeeeeeeeeeee
eeeeeeeeeeeeeeeeEEEEEEEEEEEEEE
EEEEEEEEEEEEEEEEEEEEEEEEEE ...

You've been making the amusing high-pitched whining noise for over an hour now and you're still having fun, but what you don't realise is that the amusing high-pitched whining noise coming from the end of the balloon is EXACTLY the same as a sound that drives the giant South American mosquito into a feeding frenzy. Pretty soon the house is surrounded by these huge, disgusting and extremely hungry beasts. They break through the doors and the windows, and all stick their proboscises into you. They drain every last drop of blood from your body. You die.

THE END

LETTER FROM
AUTHOR OF THIS BOOK...

19

You realise that you can't afford to waste any more time. You have barely passed halfway! You have blown up only eight balloons so far—there are still seven to go! You concentrate on the task at hand. You blow the balloon up and knot the end. That makes nine down, six to go. You pick another balloon out of the packet. You blow it up, tie the end and are suddenly dumbstruck by its beauty. It's perfect! The most perfect balloon you have ever seen! So smooth, so soft and SO round. You fall helplessly and hopelessly in love with the balloon.

*If your love story has a tragic end, go to 20.

*If you live happily ever after, go to 21.

20

You introduce your balloon to your family and declare your intention to get married. But nobody understands your love. They laugh at you. You elope. You are happy for a few hours, but then your balloon floats away with another balloon—one of those

... REGRET TO INFORM YOU...
... MUST FIRE YOU...

cute little balloon animals that you can't possibly hope to compete with. You beg your balloon to come back to you. It just laughs in your face. The cute little balloon animal beats you up. Your heart breaks. You die.

THE END

21

You introduce your balloon to your family and declare your intention to get married. But nobody understands your love. They laugh at you. You elope. You spend the happiest two hours of your life with that balloon but, in time, you both realise that nothing lasts forever. Your balloon begins to deflate. You say a tearful farewell and you both give thanks for the time you had together rather than regret the time you didn't have. The balloon loses all its air. You bury its skin and then move back home, remember what you were doing before you fell in love and then blow up another balloon. Ten down, five to go. You've just started blowing up the eleventh

... HOPELESS IDIOT... CAN'T COUNT... NOT FUNNY... ... NOT EVEN LOOK LIKE EEL ...

balloon when the mail arrives. It's a letter for you! You read it. It says:

This letter has been sent to you for good luck. The original copy is from the Netherlands. It has been around the world nine times. The luck has now been brought to you. You will receive good luck within four days of receiving this letter, provided that, in turn, you send it back out. DO NOT SEND MONEY. Do not keep this letter. It must leave your hands within ninety-six hours of you receiving it.

You must make twenty identical copies of this letter. Send it to your friends, parents, or associates. After a few days you will get a surprise. This is true even if you are not superstitious. Take note of the following.

Constantine Dino received the chain letter in 1953. He asked his secretary to make twenty copies and send them. A few days later, he won

...WILL BE REPLACED BY MECHANICAL ELECTRIC EEL...

a lottery for two million dollars in his country.

Carlo Caditt, an office employee, received the chain letter. He forgot about it and a few days later he lost his job. He then found the chain letter and sent it to twenty people. Five days later he got an even better job.

Dolon Fairchild received the chain letter and, not believing it, threw it away. Nine days later he died.

For no reason whatsoever should this chain be broken. Remember, SEND NO MONEY. Please do not ignore this. IT WORKS!

*If you ignore the letter and go on with blowing up the eleventh balloon, go to 22.
*If you ask your secretary to make twenty copies and send them, go to 23.

EH?

You ignore the letter and get on with blowing up the balloon. You break the chain. And even though you are not superstitious, bad luck! You die.

THE END

You ask your secretary to make twenty copies of the chain letter and send them. The telephone rings. It's a representative from the national lottery. He informs you that you have just won two million dollars. That's strange, you think, since you don't remember even buying a ticket. You figure it just goes to show you the power of chain letters. But then you remember that you don't have a secretary, either. That letter was NEVER copied and NEVER sent out. You broke the chain! The telephone rings again. It's another representative from the national lottery. He informs you that there's been a mistake and that you haven't won two million dollars after all. You shrug. Easy come, easy go. You go

back to blowing up the balloon. Eleven down, four to go. You've just started on the twelfth balloon when the doorbell rings.

*If you open the door, go to 24.

*If you ignore the doorbell and go on with blowing up the balloon, go to 25.

24

The doorbell rings again. 'Coming!' you call as you walk to the door and open it. It's a great white shark! It explains that it has beached itself, rolled all the way up the sand, got on a bus and travelled to your suburb, rolled all the way down your street, opened your garden gate, rolled all the way up your path and onto your doorstep, and rung your doorbell.

'But why?' you ask.

'Because I'm hungry!' it says.

'Oh,' you say. 'That would explain it, then.'

The shark lunges forward and bites you in half. You die.

TRULY SHOCKING DAYS
MAY 31, the day BIG TIMBO ate 347 jam donuts.

THE END

25

The doorbell rings again. You ignore it. You must stay focused. These balloons aren't going to blow themselves up. Besides, you never know who might be at your door. Only yesterday you read a newspaper report about a boy eaten by a shark on his own doorstep! You just can't be too careful these days. Twelve down, three to go. You blow up another balloon. You knot the end. But then a sudden gust of wind blows it out the window! You chase after it. You run up hills. You run down hills, but the balloon is always just out of reach. It floats out over a cliff. You keep running. You're running in mid-air, but not getting anywhere.

*If you look down, go to 26
*If you look up, go to 27

26

You look down and realise where you are. Unfortunately, you are three thousand metres up in the air. You fall. Luckily you hit a trampoline. You bounce up into the air again. But a gust of wind blows you slightly to the left and you fall down straight into a giant mashing and pulverising machine that is sitting just to the left of the trampoline. You are mashed and pulverised. You die.

THE END

27

You look up and see the balloon floating only centimetres above your head. You reach up and grab it. You float out over the ocean and then the wind blows you back home and safely through the open window. Thirteen down, two to go. You blow up another balloon. But then your friend Danny comes around. He sees your bag of balloons.

'Let's have a water bomb fight!' he says.

'No, Danny,' you say, 'that's not a good idea. I have to get these balloons blown up and into Jen's room as a surprise for her birthday tomorrow.'

'Spoil sport,' says Danny, and he fills a balloon with water and throws it at you. It

AMAZING NOSE TRICK #47.

SNIFF THIS SPOT FOR 30 SECONDS.

What do you smell?

For answer turn to page 62.

hits you right in the face and bursts. You are absolutely soaked.

*If you fill up a balloon with water and throw it at Danny, go to 28.

*If you tell Danny to grow up and go away, go to 29.

28

You fill up a balloon with water and throw it at Danny. It hits him in the face and drenches him. But that's not the end of the matter. He throws a second water bomb at you. You throw a second water bomb at him. You continue the fight, all the while making your water bombs bigger and bigger and bigger until you each have the equivalent of a nuclear arsenal of water bombs. You're just about to start lobbing your nuclear water bombs at each other when you realise what the consequences will be.

'Let's not be stupid about this, Danny,' you say. 'We have reached a point of mutually assured destruction. If we throw these balloons we will both die. There will be no winner ... only losers.'

'Yes, you're right,' says Danny. 'Let's not be stupid.'

He looks at you. You look at him. You throw the balloons at each other. They collide mid-air and unleash a tsunami of mind-boggling proportions. You are both swept away. Danny drowns. He dies. You drown. You die.

THE END

29

You tell Danny to grow up and go away and let you prepare your sister's birthday surprise in peace. You finish tying the balloon. Fourteen down, one to go. You pick up the last balloon and start to blow. You are incredibly fortunate. Nothing bad happens at all. Your lips don't snap off. Your face is not blown off. You are not crushed to death by adoring fans. You don't die of embarrassment. You are not decapitated by glass shattered in a sonic balloon-burst blast. Your head doesn't inflate and burst. You don't blow yourself inside out. You are not flattened by a

steamroller. You are not swept away in a cyclone. You are not sucked bloodless by a swarm of giant South American mosquitoes. You don't die of heartbreak. You don't die because you failed to make twenty copies of a chain letter. You are not eaten by a shark on your front doorstep. You don't get mashed and pulverised in a giant mashing and pulverising machine. You are not drowned in a tsunami. Nothing bad happens at all. You've done it! You have blown up fifteen pink balloons! And you are still alive!

You wait until you are sure Jen is asleep. You tie a pretty pink ribbon to each of the balloons and carry them down the hallway towards Jen's bedroom. You take a deep breath before entering. It is very dangerous to be in Jen's bedroom. The fumes from her perfume, hair gel, body spray, deodorant and nail polish are overwhelming. You quickly place the balloons all around her bed. Even though you are a boy and you have a mortal hatred of the colour pink, you have to

admit that they do look beautiful. You leave, closing the door quietly, feeling really good about what you've done. You might be an annoying little brother, but at least you are a thoughtful one.

However, all is not well. Overnight, the fumes from Jen's perfume, hair gel, body spray, deodorant and nail polish cause the balloon rubber to break down and dissolve. All the bad breath that you used to inflate the balloons gradually fills up the room and slowly but surely poisons Jen in her sleep. (If there's one thing more deadly than perfume, hair gel, body spray, deodorant and nail polish fumes, it's your bad breath!) Jen doesn't even live to see her fifteenth birthday. She dies.

In the morning, not realising the birthday girl is dead, you and your parents enter her bedroom singing 'Happy Birthday' and carrying a cake with fifteen lit candles. The flames ignite the lethally poisonous and highly flammable bad-breath gas and the room explodes. The house explodes. Your parents explode. Your dog explodes.

So much for trying to do something nice for somebody, you think. It is your last thought. YOU explode. You die.

THE END

UNFUNNIEST HOME VIDEO

Danny is at the top of the driveway, sitting on a tiny tricycle I used to ride when I was little.

He looks pretty funny.

But not as funny as he's going to look in a few minutes.

Not if everything goes according to plan.

And if everything does go according to plan, we're going to win two hundred thousand dollars from the Funniest Home Videos show for the funniest home video of the year.

Yes, you read that correctly.

TWO   HUNDRED   THOUSAND DOLLARS.

And just in case you still don't get it, that's

TWO HUNDRED THOUSAND DOLLARS!

All Danny has to do is ride down the driveway, hit a banana skin, skid out of control and then crash into the fence, and the money is ours.

'Okay, Danny,' I say. 'Ride down the driveway, hit the banana skin, skid out of control and then crash into the fence. Got that?'

'Got it,' says Danny.

I press Record on the video camera. 'Action!' I yell.

But Danny just sits there.

I press Stop.

'What's the problem?' I say. 'How come you didn't do it?'

'Are you sure this is a good idea?' says Danny.

'It's brilliant!' I say. 'Trust me—it will be the funniest bike stack ever. We'll win for sure.'

'I know,' says Danny, 'but why do I have to be the one doing it?'

'Well,' I say, 'SOMEBODY'S got to hold the camera.'

'Why can't I hold the camera and YOU ride?' says Danny.

'Because that's a stupid idea.'

'Why?'

'Because it just IS, that's why.'

'Oh,' says Danny.

Sometimes he can be a bit thick.

'All right,' I say. 'Ready?'

Danny nods.

I press Record. 'Action!' I say.

'Just one question,' says Danny. 'What's so stupid about it?'

I press Stop.

'Because I've suffered enough!' I say. 'Who was it who was almost sucked out into space because some idiot let go of the rope tied to the bunch of helium balloons that was attached to his back?'

'You,' says Danny.

'And who was it who almost got killed in a runaway pram because some idiot thought it would be funny to let the pram go at the top of a very, very steep hill?'

'You,' says Danny.

'And who was it who almost got drowned in a shower cubicle because some idiot

siliconed up all the cracks and the door and tried to fill the whole shower with water?'

'You,' says Danny. 'But that wasn't my fault. That was all your idea! I wasn't even there!'

'It doesn't matter!' I say. 'The point is that it was ME who was in danger. So I'm doing the videotaping!'

Danny thinks for a minute.

At least, I think he's thinking. He has a pained sort of look on his face. Which, as far as I know, is as close as he gets to actual thinking.

'Okay,' he finally says. 'I guess that's fair.'

'Fair?' I say. 'It's more than fair! In fact, you should be thanking me! Compared to what I've been through, riding a tricycle that skids on a banana skin and crashes into a fence is nothing.'

'You're right,' says Danny. 'Thank you, Andy, for putting me on a tricycle and giving me the opportunity to hit a banana skin, skid out of control and crash into a fence.'

AMAZING
NOSE
TRICK #47.

(Answer from p. 53)

1. You smell awful.
2. You smell a black dot.
3. YOU SMELL JUST SHOCKING!
4. YOU SMELL.
5. YOU SMELL!
6. YOU SMELL!

62

'Don't mention it,' I say.

'Just one more question,' says Danny.

'What now!?' I say.

'Wouldn't it be funnier if we put Sooty on the bike?' says Danny. 'They LOVE funny animals on that show!'

'Danny!' I say. 'I'm shocked! That's cruelty to animals!'

'Better than cruelty to ME!' he says. 'And it would be even funnier if we dressed Sooty up. Like in a ballet tutu or something.'

'No,' I say. 'It will look too set up ... but YOU in a tutu ... now that WOULD be funny!'

'No way!' says Danny.

'Well,' I say, 'if you don't want to make an easy two hundred thousand dollars, then fine ...'

'Hang on ...' says Danny. 'Why is it up to me? Why don't YOU wear the tutu?'

'Because nobody will see me—I'm behind the camera, remember?' I say. 'Now come on! We're wasting time. We have to get this finished and in the post this afternoon!'

'Okay, but NO tutu,' says Danny.

'Fine,' I say. 'It'll be funny enough. Let's

63

CLEVER
THINGS
TO DO WITH
BANANA
SKINS

USE ONE AS
A WIG.

USE THEM
AS EAR
DECORATIONS.

PUT THEM ON
YOUR HEAD,
SET THEM
ON FIRE
AND SEND
SMOKE
SIGNALS TO
YOUR FRIENDS.

just get it done. The sooner it's in, the sooner we can sit back and count our money.'

Danny sits back down on the trike.

'Action!' I say, pressing Record.

Danny rides down the driveway. But he's wobbling all over the place. He misses the banana skin, drags his feet along the ground to slow down and 'falls'—very carefully—into the fence.

'How was that?' he says

'Hopeless!' I say. 'It's meant to look like an accident! The show's called FUNNIEST Home Videos ... not FAKEST Home Videos!'

'Sorry,' says Danny, 'I'll try again.'

'No,' I say. 'It's not working. We need something better. Bigger. Funnier! Maybe if you get up on the roof.'

'The roof?' says Danny.

'Yeah!' I say. 'We'll put the banana skin on the roof.'

'What would a banana skin be doing on the roof?'

'I don't know,' I say. 'It will just be funny, that's all.'

'But I could get hurt!' says Danny.

'Not if you fall right,' I say. 'Do that sort of, you know, that sort of roll that professional stuntmen do.'

'You mean that sort of roll that professional stuntmen go to professional stuntman school to learn?' says Danny.

'Yeah,' I say, 'that one.'

'You're forgetting one thing,' says Danny. 'Two things, actually.'

'What?'

'One: I'm not a professional stuntman,' he says. 'And two: I haven't been to professional stuntman school!'

'Okay,' I say, 'how about I put the trampoline underneath you? You won't get hurt, then.'

'But I'll just bounce off,' says Danny. 'And THEN I'll get hurt.'

'Maybe, but think how funny it will be!' I say. 'A bike stack and a trampoline accident in one shot! We'll win for sure!'

'Yeah, but I could get seriously hurt!' says Danny.

'Perhaps,' I say, 'but you'll be rich. You'll be able to afford the best medical treatment one hundred thousand dollars can buy.'

SHOCKING PLACES TO HIDE

(BOO)

IN YOUR MUM'S HANDBAG.

(BOO)

IN THE DRYER.

(BOO.)

IN THE DOG.

'I thought you said it was **TWO** hundred thousand dollars,' he says.

'It is,' I remind him. 'But half is mine.'

'Half?' he says. 'But I'm taking all the risk!'

'Yes, but it was MY idea,' I say.

'Yeah, but ...'

'So you'll do it?' I say. 'Because if you don't want to do it, there are plenty of others who will.'

'Like who?' he says. 'Who would be stupid enough?'

The answer is nobody, of course. Nobody is stupider than Danny.

'I can think of heaps of people who'd jump at the chance,' I lie. 'But I'm giving you first choice. So do you want to do it or not?'

Danny shrugs. 'Okay.'

'Great!' I say. I fetch the ladder from the shed, prop it up against the side of the house and drag the trampoline closer. 'Get your clothes off and I'll give you a boost up.'

'Hang on,' says Danny. 'Did you say "clothes off"?'

'Yeah,' I say. 'At least your pants. It will be funnier if you've got no pants on.'

'No way!' he says.

'Trust me!' I say. 'When somebody's pants fall down or their dress gets ripped off, it's really funny. So we'll be combining danger and no clothes! We can't lose!'

'I'll climb on the roof,' says Danny, 'but I'm keeping my pants on.'

'Fine!' I say. 'But if we don't win, we'll both know why.'

Danny starts climbing the ladder.

He gets halfway up when he stops and turns around. 'There's a kitten,' he says, pointing behind me.

I turn around.

'Oh, yeah,' I say. 'It belongs to our neighbours. It's always coming over here. Ignore it.'

'But it's so cute!' says Danny, climbing down the ladder.

'Danny!' I say. 'What about the video?'

'But it's a kitten! And it's so cute!' he says. 'Look at its cute little face!'

'Danny!' I say. 'There are two hundred thousand dollars at stake here and you just

THE DANGERS OF THE KITTEN

KITTENS SEEM SO INNOCENT, YET WHILE YOU SLEEP THEY PLOT...

TO SMOTHER YOU.

TO GAS YOU IN THE OVEN.

TO PUSH YOU OVER A CLIFF.

want to stare at some dumb kitten's face?'

Danny picks the kitten up and holds it close to his chest.

'Hello, cutie,' he says. 'What's your name? I think I'll call you Fluffy. Because you're SO fluffy!'

I don't know how much more of this I can take.

In fact, I don't know how much more of this the kitten can take.

Now Danny's touching noses with it.

'Danny, do you realise cats have a lot of germs?'

'Not Fluffy!' says Danny, burying his face in its fur. 'You wouldn't have any germs, would you?' he says to the kitten.

Right. That's it.

I put the camera down.

I grab the kitten from Danny's arms and put it on the ground.

'Get!' I shout, stamping my foot.

It runs away.

'That was mean,' says Danny.

'Oh for goodness sakes, Danny,' I say. 'As soon as we get this video done I'll find the kitten and apologise. And when we win the

BAD
LITTLE
KITTENS

money I'll buy it a diamond-studded collar. Will that make you happy?'

'It would make Fluffy happy,' says Danny.

'Good,' I say. 'Now get up on that roof!'

'I don't like this game any more,' says Danny.

'It's not a game!' I remind him. 'It's work. And we're getting paid two hundred thousand dollars for it!'

Danny shrugs and starts climbing the ladder.

He climbs carefully from the ladder onto the roof.

I'm about to pass the tricycle up to him when we hear a loud, high-pitched noise.

'What's that?' says Danny.

'What's what?'

'It's coming from that tree,' says Danny.

'Ignore it,' I say.

'I can't,' says Danny, looking up into the branches. 'Look! Fluffy is stuck in the tree! She must have run up there when you scared her.'

'Well, let's hope that teaches her a lesson,' I say.

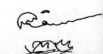

'But we can't just leave her there,' says Danny.

'Why not?' I say. 'She'll be okay. She can catch birds.'

'But she can't get down!' says Danny. He starts climbing back down the ladder. 'We have to save her!'

'Have you gone mad?' I say. 'What about our video?'

'I can't help it if I love kittens,' says Danny, picking up the ladder and carrying it towards the tree. 'Just look at her sad little face!'

'Danny,' I say, 'could you stop talking like that? You're making me feel sick!'

Danny stops talking, but he's got a crazy look in his eyes.

He puts the ladder against the tree.

As I watch him try to steady it an idea begins to form.

Little kittens grow into BIG CATS.

Kitten ...

ladder ...

tree ...

idiot ...

ladder ...

tree ...

tree ...

ladder ...

kitten ...

idiot ...

idiot ... on ladder ... up tree ... AND a kitten ...

If Danny were to fall out of that tree ... we might just get our funniest home video after all.

And if the kitten were to fall as well ... wow! I've seen plenty of people fall off ladders on Funniest Home Videos, but never a kitten! And NEVER both a person and a kitten at the same time.

This could be the funniest home video EVER!

In fact, how can it fail? After all, what goes up, must come down.

I'll offer to hold the ladder for Danny as he climbs, and then once he's up I'll adjust it so it's sure to fall as he climbs down.

Yes, I know what you're thinking. You're thinking that you shouldn't do that to your best friend. But don't forget, we are talking about two hundred thousand dollars.

TWO HUNDRED THOUSAND DOLLARS!

TWO HUNDRED THOUSAND DOLLARS!!!

I'll be doing it for his own good ... he'll thank me for it later.

Besides, it's not like he'll get hurt. Not really. The ground is pretty soft. There's plenty of grass. And he's not up THAT high. Some of those falls on Funniest Home Videos are MUCH higher. And those people are okay. Well, presumably. And cats, well, they can fall out of 100-storey skyscrapers and not hurt themselves. And they have nine lives. So even if it dies it will STILL be alive.

Fluffy miaows again.

And again.

And again.

'Hang on, Danny,' I say. 'I'll hold the ladder so you don't fall and hurt yourself.'

'Thanks, Andy,' says Danny. 'You're a true friend.'

And he's right.

Sort of.

Fluffy miaows again.

Danny starts climbing the ladder. 'Coming, Fluffy!' he calls.

The ladder wobbles, but I hold it steady.

Danny reaches the top of the ladder, but Fluffy is up very high, still well out of his reach.

'Here, kitty, kitty,' says Danny, climbing off the ladder up into the tree.

Here's my chance.

I reposition the ladder so that one of its legs is resting on a tree root.

The moment Danny puts his full weight on it the ladder will be sure to topple sideways.

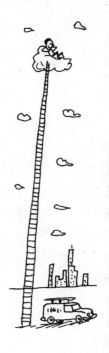

I push Record on the camera and step back.

This is going to be great.

In fact, this is going to be MORE than great.

This is going to make us rich!

'How are you going, Danny?' I call.

'I've got her!' he calls from the top of the tree.

'So what are you waiting for?' I say. 'Come down!'

'Coming,' he says.

 73

'Be careful!' I say. And then I whisper, 'Not!'

I can hardly wait.

Any moment now ...

I check that the video is recording.

It is.

But I'm too excited.

My hands are trembling.

This is no good.

It will ruin the video!

I sit down on the grass and steady the camera by resting my elbows on my knees.

I take a deep breath and stare intently into the viewfinder.

Action!

Finally a leg appears through the leaves.

Then another.

Danny's left foot touches the top rung of the ladder.

It wobbles violently.

But somehow Danny manages to steady it and plant his other foot on it as well.

Then he steps his right foot down onto the next rung of the ladder.

Here we go!

The ladder lurches sideways.

74

Danny panics.

And screams.

He tries to grab a tree branch, fails, and kicks against the trunk instead.

This causes the ladder to start to fall backwards, instead of sideways as I'd hoped.

Danny is at the top of the falling ladder, one hand holding the kitten, the other hand waving wildly in the air. Well, actually, the hand holding the kitten is waving wildly too, and miaowing.

The ladder ...

Danny ...

and that stupid kitten ...

all falling backwards through the air ...

uh-oh ...

falling ...

straight ...

towards ...

me!

I close my eyes.

WHAM!

The impact knocks the video camera out of my hand.

I hear a sickening crunch.

Oh no, I hope that's not my skull.

MORE DANGERS OF THE KITTEN

KITTENS SEEM SO INNOCENT, YET WHILE YOU SLEEP THEY PLOT...

TO CHOP YOU TO BITS.

TO MULCH YOU.

TO BLAST YOU INTO SPACE.

75 BLPZ9OKL!

But I guess it can't be, otherwise I couldn't be hoping that it wasn't my skull.

Oh no … what if it was Danny's skull?

What if I've just murdered my best friend?

Murdered my best friend for a lousy one hundred thousand dollars?

Well, technically I guess I would get the whole two hundred thousand dollars if Danny were dead.

Wait a minute!

What am I thinking?

What's happening to me?

How could I be so greedy?

So heartless?

He's my best friend!

I'm too scared to open my eyes.

But then I have another thought.

Not only have I just filmed a Funniest Home Videos first—a person AND a kitten falling off a ladder, but they hit the camera as well!

That's the absolute icing on the cake of a funny home video!

It's the BEST possible thing that could have happened!

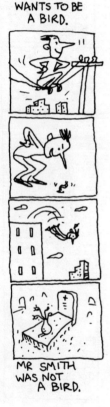

MR SMITH
WANTS TO BE
A BIRD.

MR SMITH
WAS NOT
A BIRD.

FLMKWPP!

76

'Andy?' says Danny.

'Danny?' I say. 'You're alive?'

'Yes,' he says.

'Your skull didn't get smashed in?' I say.

'No,' he says. 'But I think I might have squashed Fluffy.'

Fluffy miaows.

'No, I think she's okay,' I say. I open my eyes.

We're all lying in a sprawled heap on the grass beside the ladder, which landed on the concrete path.

Me, Danny and Fluffy.

'Ouch!' says Danny. 'That hurt!'

'You can say that again,' I say. 'But don't worry, it will be worth it. I filmed the whole thing.'

'You ... filmed ... it?' says Danny.

'Yes,' I say. 'It was brilliant. You and Fluffy falling out of the tree and then, as if that wasn't funny enough already, you hit the camera ... it was a classic!'

'But how could you have done that?' he says. 'Weren't you holding the ladder?'

'No,' I say. 'I couldn't hold the ladder and film you at the same time.'

TODAY NOTHING IS FUNNY.

NOT OLD MEN SLIPPING ON BANANA PEELS.

NOR PRINCIPALS WHOSE PANTS FALL DOWN DURING ASSEMBLY.

AND CERTAINLY NOT DOGS WHO SNIFF EACH OTHER'S BUMS SO CLOSELY THEY GET STUCK.

'But if you'd been holding the ladder I wouldn't have fallen!' says Danny.

'And if you hadn't fallen I wouldn't have had anything to film!' I point out. 'And we wouldn't be in the running to win two hundred thousand dollars.'

I look around for the camera to show Danny the footage. When he sees it he will understand why NOT holding the ladder was such a good idea.

That's when I see it.

Lying there on the path, underneath the ladder.

The video camera.

The lens is broken.

The shell is crushed and sitting in a puddle of plastic buttons, metal strips and digital video tape.

Whatever brilliant, funny home video I just filmed is never going to be seen by anybody ... that's for sure.

'I can't believe it,' I say. 'The camera's broken! We didn't get the video! Best funniest home video ever, except that it's not on video!'

'Oh yes it is,' says a voice above us.

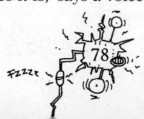

FZZZt

We look up.

It's Jen. With her new mobile phone. Her new mobile phone that has everything … including a video camera!

'I got the whole thing!' she says. 'And I'm going to win two hundred thousand dollars from Funniest Home Videos, thanks to you two idiots! That was definitely the funniest accident I've ever seen!'

'But that's OUR accident!' I say.

'MY accident, actually,' says Danny.

'Yes, but it's MY video!' says Jen.

'But that's not fair,' I say. 'It was MY idea! I'm the one who put the ladder on the tree root so that it would fall.'

'Thanks a lot, FRIEND,' says Danny, giving me a dirty look.

'And thanks for the confession!' says Jen. 'I'm still filming, you know. And Mum and Dad are going to be very interested to hear you admit that it was all YOUR fault that the video camera got broken. So long, losers!'

She goes inside.

'I can't believe it!' I say. 'Not only did Jen just steal our two hundred thousand

dollars, but Mum and Dad are going to kill me for wrecking the video camera. And, as if that wasn't bad enough, now we're going to look like a pair of idiots on prime time television.'

'Look on the bright side,' says Danny.

'Bright side?' I say. 'There is no bright side!'

'Yes, there is,' says Danny. 'We saved Fluffy, didn't we?'

I shake my head.

Fluffy.

Hmmm …

Hang on …

Fluffy …

That gives me an idea …

I wonder what Fluffy would look like in a tutu …

on a bike …

going down a hill …

'Hey, Danny,' I say. 'Do your parents have a video camera?'

'Yeah,' he says.

'Do you think we could borrow it?' I say.

'I suppose so,' says Danny. 'But if you're planning to make another video, you can

just forget it. There's no way I'm going to be in it.'

'Don't worry, you don't have to be,' I say. 'Here, Fluffy. Here, kitty, kitty, kitty ...'

101 Really dangerous things

(and twelve truly shocking facts)

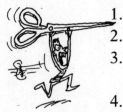

1. Running with scissors.
2. Running while eating.
3. Running while eating a pair of scissors.
4. Asking somebody on the other side of the room to throw you a pair of scissors.
5. Running screaming out of the room and across a busy road without looking because you have a pair of scissors stuck in your eye.

6. Whacking your sister with a pillow and she pulls a fork out of her pyjamas.
7. Whacking your sister with a pillow and she pulls an atomic bomb out of her pyjamas.
8. Looking into the end of a hose to see why the water is not coming out.
9. Looking into the barrel of a popgun to see why the cork is not coming out.
10. Touching electric fences.
11. Weeing on electric fences.
12. Chasing cars and trying to bite their tyres. (My dog, Sooty, does this.)
13. Putting your hands out of the window of a moving car.
14. Sitting behind the driver of a moving car, putting your hands over their eyes, and yelling 'GUESS WHO?'
15. Climbing out onto the roof of a moving car, lowering yourself down onto the windscreen and waving at the driver.
16. Picking your nose with a pencil.

SHOCKING GENETIC MIX-UPS #1.

MUFFLER MOOSE

17. Picking your nose with a pencil while running.

18. Picking your nose with a pencil while riding in a car travelling down a really bumpy road.

19. Pressing little red buttons that say, 'DO NOT PRESS THIS LITTLE RED BUTTON OR THE WHOLE UNIVERSE WILL EXPLODE!'

20. Eating a whole can of baked beans.

21. Playing with matches.

22. Playing with matches after eating a whole can of baked beans.

23. Jumping on trampolines.

24. Jumping on trampolines after eating a whole can of baked beans.

25. Doing a really high bounce on a trampoline. Especially when, while you are up in the air, some IDIOT, for example, Danny Pickett, comes along and moves the trampoline.

26. Moving the trampoline back to where it's supposed to be and forgetting that you left a rake lying on the ground, stepping on it and getting smacked in the face with the rake handle.

27. Flicking rubber bands at your friends.

28. Flicking giant rubber bands at your friends.

29. Having giant rubber bands flicked at you by your friends who are sick and tired of you flicking giant rubber bands at them.

30. Germs.

31. Girl germs. (Shocking fact #1: Girl germs have been scientifically proven—by me and my best friend, Danny—to be the most dangerous germs on the planet. Anybody who has ever TOUCHED a girl, been in the SAME ROOM as a girl or even THOUGHT about a girl should immediately run to the nearest hospital before it is too late. Anybody who IS a girl, well, bad luck. It already IS too late. You are doomed.)

32. Boy germs. Actually, no. That's just a joke. (Shocking fact #2: Not only are boy germs completely harmless, they have been scientifically proven—by

 85

me and my best friend, Danny—to
be GOOD for you.)

33. Waving red capes at charging bulls
with really big, sharp horns sticking
out of their heads.

34. Waving red capes at charging bulls
with really big, sharp scissors
sticking out of their heads where
their horns should be.

35. Letting your best friend push
you around in a pram and then
discovering that he is NOT your best
friend because he takes you to the
top of a really steep hill and lets go
of the pram.

36. Standing in a shower, putting your
foot over the plughole and trying to
fill the whole cubicle up with water.
Especially when there are big cracks
in between the doors, and the water
leaks out, goes all over the floor
and fills up the bathroom, and then
your parents open the door and get
washed down the hallway, out the
front door and down the street by an
enormous tidal wave which, as well

as drowning your parents, drowns half the neighbourhood.

37. Zippers. Especially on trousers. (Shocking fact #3: According to National Injury Surveillance Unit statistics, trouser-zip injuries are the leading cause of clothing-related injury. A spokesperson recommended that boys and men use button flies instead.)

38. Buttons. (Shocking fact #4: According to National Injury Surveillance Unit statistics, many children are hospitalised every year as a result of inserting buttons up their noses.)

39. Danny's socks. He hasn't changed them for two and a half years. (Shocking fact #5: According to National Injury Surveillance Unit statistics, the last time Danny took his socks off, ten people died immediately. Hundreds more were rushed to hospital suffering bruised nostrils and a variety of serious breathing difficulties.)

The Night of the GIANT MUTANT KILLER SOCK

STENCH CLOUD

40. Removing the head of your sister's favourite Barbie doll and then your sister catching you and trying to remove YOUR head.

41. Headless Barbie dolls that come alive in the middle of the night and chase you around the house with scissors in their hands.

SHOCKING
GENETIC
MIX-UPS
#2.

MUFFLER
MoSQUITO

42. Getting all the chemicals in your chemistry set, mixing them together and drinking them.

43. Discovering, after drinking the contents of your chemistry set, that you have X-ray vision—which allows you to see through people's clothing—and then accidentally looking at your brother or sister.

44. Or your parents.

45. Or your teacher!

46. Running out of the room screaming and across a busy road without looking because you just saw your brother or your sister or your parents or your teacher in the nude.

47. Riding a bike down a really steep hill without holding onto the handlebars.

48. Riding a bike down a really steep hill without holding onto the handlebars, with your eyes shut.

49. Riding a bike down a really steep hill without holding onto the handlebars, with your eyes shut and WITHOUT your helmet on.

50. Chairs. Especially when some IDIOT, for example, Danny Pickett, pulls a chair away just as you are about to sit down on it.

51. Thumbtacks. Especially when some IDIOT, for example, Danny Pickett, leaves one on your chair for a joke and you sit on it and the pain makes you jump up so high that you hit your head on the ceiling with such force that you put a big crack in the plaster.

52. Falling chunks of ceiling plaster that crush you to death.

53. Sitting on top of a flesh-eating ants' nest.

54. Sitting on top of a flesh-eating ants' nest in the nude.

55. Toasting marshmallows with a

long stick and accidentally poking somebody in the eye with the stick, and then toasting their eyeball instead and not even realising until you're halfway through eating it.

56. Hacking your way through the jungle with a machete and realising you're not actually in the jungle—you're in your house—well, what's left of your house—because you've just hacked it, and everything inside it, to pieces.

57. And you hear your parents opening what's left of the front door and coming inside.

58. And when they see what you've done they get REALLY MAD!

59. AND THEY'VE GOT MACHETES IN THEIR HANDS!!!

60. Staple guns that go out of control and chase you around the house.

61. Parents that go out of control and chase you around the house with machetes.

62. Forgetting to hold your breath when you walk past a cemetery.

63. Forgetting to hold your breath when you walk past your sister's room. (See number 31 on this list.)
64. Forgetting to start breathing again after you've walked past a cemetery or your sister's room.
65. Invasions of aliens from other planets.
66. Invasions of scissors from other planets.
67. Each person in the world eating a can of baked beans on the same day. (Shocking fact #6: A mass consumption of baked beans of this magnitude would create such an overwhelming surge of methane that the protective layers of the Earth's atmosphere would be instantly destroyed and all the fresh air in the world would rush out into space and all life on Earth would be instantly suffocated ... even the fish.)
68. Inventing a time machine, travelling back in time and accidentally landing the time machine on top of your grandmother when she's only a little girl and killing her dead,

which means that she would never have been able to grow up, which means that she could never have had children, which means that your mother—or your father—depending on which grandmother you just killed—could never have been born, which means that YOU could never have been born.

69. Thinking about time travel. It doesn't make any sense. Because if you had never been born, how could you have invented a time machine and gone back in time to squash your grandmother in the first place? (Shocking fact #7: People who think too much about this stuff end up blowing the little light bulb in their brains and then they can't think properly any more and end up doing really dangerous things like inventing time machines and travelling back in time and accidentally landing on top of their grandmothers and killing them dead ...)

70. Your grandmother inventing a time

92

machine and travelling into the future and accidentally landing on top of YOU and killing YOU dead.

71. Playing with poisonous spiders. Especially when they get into your pyjamas and you can't find them.

72. Playing with loaded mouse traps. Especially when they get into your pyjamas and you can't find them. Especially if you are a boy.

73. Dreaming that you are running barefoot through a room full of loaded mouse traps and then waking up and realising that you ARE running barefoot through a room full of loaded mouse traps.

74. Digging holes. Especially when you are right next to the water at the beach and some IDIOT, for example, Danny Pickett, tells you to get into the hole and then buries you up to your neck in sand and leaves you there ... just as the tide is coming in.

75. Playing with things that live in holes: for example, flesh-eating ants, spiders, snakes, your sister.

THE TRUE STORY OF MUFFLER DUCK

A POOR LOST MUFFLER WANDERS THROUGH THE CITY.

HUNGRY AND TRUCKLESS HE BUSKS FOR A MEAL.

BUT ALL HE EARNS ARE BOTTLE TOPS.

SAD AND ALONE, HE DECIDES TO END IT ALL...

(Cont' Page 145.)

76. Digging really deep holes that are so deep they go right down to the centre of the Earth. (Shocking fact #8: The temperature at the centre of the Earth is 5500 °C—almost as hot as the Sun!)

77. Standing at the edge of a really deep hole. Especially when some IDIOT, for example, Danny Pickett, comes up behind you and shouts, 'BOO!'

78. Black holes. (Shocking fact #9: Black holes are the most dangerous and destructive force in the entire universe. If you see one coming, don't panic—just RUN!)

79. Jumping out of a plane without a parachute.

80. Jumping out of a plane WITH a parachute, but over shark-infested waters.

81. Jumping out of a plane with a shark-infested parachute.

82. Getting a bicycle pump, inserting the end into your mouth and pumping your head up until it gets so big that it explodes.

83. Looking at the sun.

84. Touching the sun.
85. Using a vacuum cleaner to remove a bandaid that's been stuck to your skin for more than six months, especially when the bandaid is really close to your eye.
86. Falling rocks. Especially when they are falling from outer space and they penetrate the upper layers of the Earth's atmosphere and hurtle down at incredible speed and land right on top of your head.
87. Paper. (Shocking fact #10: Scientific studies have shown that paper cuts are the most painful injury it is possible to inflict on yourself ... even more painful than trying to remove bandaids that have been stuck to your skin for six months or getting your eyeball sucked out of your skull by a vacuum cleaner.)

88. Playing the game called 'Scissors, Paper, Rock' with your friends, because rocks and paper are bad enough, but scissors, as I have already mentioned, are REALLY

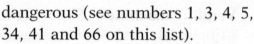

dangerous (see numbers 1, 3, 4, 5, 34, 41 and 66 on this list).

89. Jumping off a really high diving board with a really heavy anchor tied to your ankle, especially if it's less than half an hour after a really big meal.

90. Diving off a really high diving board. Especially when, while you're diving, some IDIOT, for example, Danny Pickett, comes along and drains all the water out of the swimming pool.

91. Swimming with sharks. Especially the ones with really big sharp teeth.

92. Falling coconuts. (Shocking fact #11: One hundred and fifty people are killed by falling coconuts each year. Falling coconuts kill fifteen times more people than sharks do.)

93. Falling sharks. Although much rarer than falling coconuts, they are still extremely dangerous, especially if they are falling headfirst.

94. Coconut attacks. Although still relatively rare, they are on the increase.

95. Vending machines. (Shocking fact #12: Toppled vending machines have caused at least thirty-five deaths and 140 injuries in the last twenty years.)

96. Escalators. Failing to jump off at exactly the right moment can cause your toes and then your legs and then your whole body to be sucked into the escalator and turned into mince meat. It is estimated that thousands of unwary shoppers disappear in this manner every year.

97. Swinging. Especially swinging too high.

98. Swinging too high. Especially when some IDIOT, for example, Danny Pickett, is pushing you really hard.

99. Swinging too high. Especially when some IDIOT, for example, Danny Pickett, is pushing you really hard and you yell, 'Hey, slow down!' and then you discover that your best friend is NOT really your best friend after all because he doesn't stop pushing so hard—he actually pushes harder—and you can't hold on any

97

SHOCKING
DRAWING
(from page 133)

longer and you lose your grip and go flying off the swing, up through the clouds, out into space and into orbit—which, without a spacesuit, is dangerous enough—until you slow down, that is, and re-enter the Earth's atmosphere and start falling towards the ground at close to 200 kilometres per hour without a parachute—pretty much one of the most dangerous things you can do in the whole world—but just when you think things can't possibly get any more dangerous, they DO because the friction of your body travelling so fast through the air causes your hair to catch on fire, and while you're trying to put your hair out the fire catches onto your clothes and they burn up completely so now you're falling through the air completely naked—which is a surprisingly nice feeling, except for the fact that all the people in the passing jumbo jets look out their windows and point and laugh and take photos of you

ME GET OLD JOB BACK.

98

as you plummet past them—and,
of course, for the fact that you're
falling towards the ground at close
to 200 kilometres per hour without a
parachute—but then you remember
that, fortunately, you have a
swimming pool in your backyard and
that, even more fortunately, you are
the school high-diving champion and
you're thinking, hey, this is GREAT
because now you can break the
world high-diving record, and you
get in position and begin performing
a very show-offy quadruple-tuck
reverse-twist 300-somersault 200-
kilometre-per-hour dive with triple
pike and you've almost completed
it when you realise you're not going
to be able to because the pool is
only a paddle pool—less than 15
centimetres deep—and you can't dive
headfirst into a paddle pool less than
15 centimetres deep—because that's
REALLY dangerous—so you have to
go belly first—which hurts, of course,
because not only does your belly split

ME BEST
PAGE NUMBER
EEL EVER.

open, but your body crashes through the bottom of the pool, through the outer crust of the Earth, through the rocky mantle and straight into the inner core with such force that the impact causes the entire planet to blow apart into millions of tiny chunks, killing everything and everybody, and especially you.

100. Setting fire to the paper that this list is written on and putting it down your underpants.

101. Running out of the room screaming and across a busy road without looking because your underpants are on fire because some **IDIOT**, for example, **YOU**, did number 100 on this list.

A REALLY, REALLY GOOD EXCUSE

MRS JONES
WANTS TO
BE A
TOASTER.

I run up the steps.

I throw my bag on the hook.

I rush into the classroom.

Mr Dobson is talking to the class.

He stops and turns towards me.

Everybody stares.

'You're late!' he says. 'Again! What's your excuse today?'

I take a deep breath. 'Well ...' I say.

'No!' says Mr Dobson. 'Don't tell me. Let me guess. Your mother's car had a flat tyre?'

'No, sir,' I say. 'That was last week.'

'Oh yes,' he says, thoughtfully. 'Well, then, perhaps your grandfather choked on a cornflake and you had to take him to hospital?'

MRS JONES
WAS NOT A
TOASTER.

ME BURNING TO DEATH!

101

'No, sir,' I say. 'That happened yesterday.'

'Well, what?' says Mr Dobson. 'Surely not another natural disaster? So far this term we've had a volcanic eruption, an earthquake, a tsunami, a cyclone and a willy-willy.'

Some of the boys start laughing.

'I fail to see what is so funny about willy-willies!' says Mr Dobson. 'They may be mostly harmless whirlwinds of dust, but rare ones can be large enough to threaten both people and property!'

Everybody in the class is laughing now, but Mr Dobson just shakes his head and turns his attention back to me.

'So, Andy,' he says, 'given the list of calamities that have caused you to be late so many times this term, I can hardly think what other misfortune could possibly have befallen you. But let's hear it anyway.'

'Well,' I say, taking a deep breath, 'it's kind of embarrassing.'

'Never mind,' says Mr Dobson. 'Out with it.'

I nod. 'Tight underpants,' I say.

There is a fresh burst of laughter from the class.

WATER! WATER!

Even Mr Dobson is smiling. 'Tight underpants?' he says. He sits down in his chair, and places his chalk on the table. He crosses his arms and stretches out his legs. 'Now THIS I've GOT to hear. Do tell me how a pair of tight underpants could make you THIS late for school.'

'It all started with my alarm clock,' I say. 'It didn't go off, so I woke up really late. I got dressed and rushed out of the house, eating a bowl of Choco-pops as I ran. I was almost to the end of the street when Mum called me back just to remind me to come home straight after school because I've got a dentist's appointment. "Now, don't forget," she said, "because if we're even ten minutes late they count it as a cancellation, but you still have to pay for the appointment. So if you're late I swear I'll pull that tooth out myself with a pair of pliers." And I said, "All right, Mum. I'll be there. I promise."'

'Well, this is all very interesting, Andy,' says Mr Dobson, 'but I don't see what it has to do with tight underpants.'

'Yeah, sorry,' I say, 'but that's where it

gets complicated. Do you mind if I use the blackboard?'

'Be my guest,' says Mr Dobson.

I pick up a pointer and a piece of chalk. 'Well,' I say …

I WAS HALFWAY TO SCHOOL WHEN I BECAME AWARE OF THE SYMPTOMS …

DIFFICULTY WALKING …

ZAP!

NO! FIRE HOSE STORY PAGE 1

DIFFICULTY BREATHING ...

BUT MOST OF ALL, AN UNBEARABLE BURNING PAIN AROUND MY HIPS ...

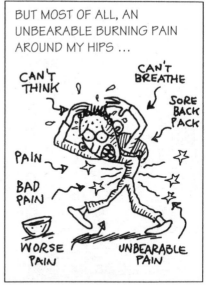

MY UNDERPANTS WERE TOO TIGHT!

I WAS REALLY SCARED.

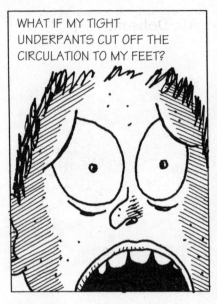

WHAT IF MY TIGHT UNDERPANTS CUT OFF THE CIRCULATION TO MY FEET?

WHAT IF THEY CUT OFF THE CIRCULATION TO MY LEGS?

BUT WORST OF ALL, WHAT IF THEY CUT OFF THE CIRCULATION TO MY ...

106

'Yes, we get the idea!' says Mr Dobson, 'there's no need to say it.'

'... brain,' I say.

'Oh,' says Mr Dobson. 'That's all right, then. I thought you were going to say ... well, never mind. Carry on.'

I TRIED TO PUT MY HAND UNDER THE WAISTBAND OF MY UNDIES BUT THEY WERE SO TIGHT I COULDN'T GET MY FINGER BETWEEN THE ELASTIC AND MY SKIN.

THEN I REMEMBERED I STILL HAD THE TEASPOON I'D USED TO EAT MY CHOCO-POPS.

I TOOK MY TROUSERS OFF AND SLID THE TEASPOON UNDER THE WAISTBAND OF MY UNDIES ...

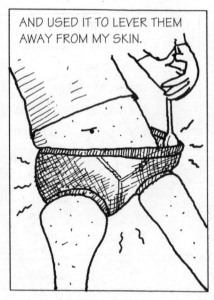

AND USED IT TO LEVER THEM AWAY FROM MY SKIN.

AHHH! FOR A MOMENT I HAD SOME RELIEF ...

BUT THE PRESSURE OF MY UNDIES WAS TOO GREAT AND THE TEASPOON SNAPPED IN HALF!

SNAP!

STICK BURNING TAIL IN HOSE

NOW THE SITUATION WAS REALLY SERIOUS!

⊗ DAILY BAD NEWS

SITUATION **REALLY** SERIOUS

I PUT THE BROKEN PIECES OF THE TEASPOON IN MY BAG AND DECIDED I HAD NO CHOICE BUT TO GO HOME, CUT MY UNDIES OFF AND CHANGE INTO A LARGER PAIR.

◄ HOME

SCHOOL ►

BUT WHEN I GOT THERE THE HOUSE WAS LOCKED AND NOBODY WAS HOME.

HOUSE LOCKED

↖ NO ONE HOME

AND THE SPARE KEY WASN'T UNDER THE BRICK WHERE IT WAS SUPPOSED TO BE.

NO KEY!

109

HEE. HEE.

THERE WAS ONLY ONE WAY IN: AN OPEN WINDOW UPSTAIRS.

I BEGAN CLIMBING—WITH GREAT DIFFICULTY—UP THE DRAINPIPE.

I WAS ALMOST AT THE TOP WHEN I HEARD SOMEONE YELL, 'HEY, YOU, GET DOWN OR I'LL CALL THE POLICE!'

HEY, YOU !!

'MIND YOUR OWN BUSINESS!' I YELLED BACK.

Get me the Police!

CLEVER EEL STOP WATER

WITHIN MINUTES THE HOUSE WAS SURROUNDED BY POLICE.

'COME DOWN OR ELSE!' SAID THE POLICE CHIEF THROUGH A MEGAPHONE.

I CLIMBED BACK DOWN AND TRIED TO EXPLAIN THAT IT WAS MY HOUSE AND THAT MY UNDIES WERE TOO TIGHT BUT THE POLICE JUST LAUGHED.

'TIGHT UNDIES ARE NO LAUGHING MATTER!' I YELLED.

'TELL IT TO THE JUDGE,' SAID THE CHIEF.

THEY TOOK ME BACK TO THE STATION AND LOCKED ME IN A CELL.

THE SITUATION WAS HOPELESS. MY UNDIES WERE TIGHTER THAN EVER. I STARTED TO CRY.

'QUIT IT, YOU LITTLE SOOK, OR I'LL REALLY GIVE YOU SOMETHING TO CRY ABOUT,' SAID A ROUGH VOICE FROM THE BACK OF THE CELL.

'WHAT COULD YOU DO TO ME THAT WOULD BE WORSE THAN HAVING A PAIR OF UNDIES THAT ARE SO TIGHT I CAN'T EVEN GET THEM OFF WITH A TEASPOON?' I SAID, PEERING INTO THE DARKNESS.

'TEASPOON?' SAID THE OWNER OF THE VOICE, AS HE EMERGED FROM THE SHADOWS. 'DID YOU SAY "TEASPOON"?'

I GASPED. IT WAS SQUIZZY 'TEASPOON' TAYLOR, A CRIMINAL MASTERMIND FAMOUS FOR DIGGING HIS WAY OUT OF HIGH-SECURITY PRISONS ALL OVER THE WORLD USING NOTHING BUT A TEASPOON!

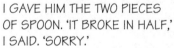

DAILY BAD NEWS

SQUIZZY 'TEASPOON' TAYLOR DIGS OUT OF JAIL AGAIN

'HAND OVER THE SPOON, KID,' HE SAID, 'AND I'LL HAVE US OUT OF HERE IN NO TIME.'

I GAVE HIM THE TWO PIECES OF SPOON. 'IT BROKE IN HALF,' I SAID. 'SORRY.'

'NO PROBLEM, KID,' SAID SQUIZZY. 'ONE HALF FOR EACH HAND. I'LL BE ABLE TO DIG TWICE AS FAST.'

SURE ENOUGH, SQUIZZY LIVED UP TO HIS REPUTATION. THAT GUY SURE KNEW HOW TO USE A TEASPOON!

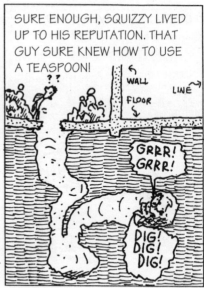

WITHIN MINUTES HE HAD TUNNELLED THROUGH THE CELL FLOOR, UNDER THE WALL AND OUT THE OTHER SIDE.

'THANKS A MILLION, SQUIZZY,' I SAID.

'COULDN'T HAVE DONE IT WITHOUT YOU, KID,' HE SAID. 'HOW ABOUT JOINING MY GANG?'

'I CAN'T,' I SAID. 'I'VE GOT TO CHANGE MY UNDIES AND THEN GET TO SCHOOL.'

'SCHOOL?' SAID SQUIZZY. 'SCHOOL'S FOR FOOLS! AND BESIDES, NOBODY SAYS NO TO SQUIZZY TAYLOR. NOBODY STILL LIVING, THAT IS, IF YOU GET MY DRIFT.'

I GOT HIS DRIFT, ALL RIGHT. IF MY TIGHT UNDIES DIDN'T KILL ME, THEN SQUIZZY CERTAINLY WOULD.

HE TOOK ME BACK TO HIS INTERNATIONAL CRIME LAIR.

INTERNATIONAL CRIME LAIR

CRIME INC.

115

CAN'T TAKE TAIL OUT OF HOSE

HE INTRODUCED ME TO HIS GANG OF CRIMINAL MASTERMIND PALS, WHO WERE PUTTING THE FINISHING TOUCHES TO AN EVIL UNDERPANTS-SHRINKING MACHINE.

THEY PLANNED TO USE IT TO SHRINK THE UNDERPANTS OF ALL THE POLICE IN THE ENTIRE WORLD AT THE EXACT SAME TIME!

THE PLAN *

* EVIL

'BUT WHY?' I SAID. 'TIGHT UNDIES ARE HORRIBLE. THEY ARE REALLY PAINFUL, AND THEY CAN CUT OFF THE CIRCULATION TO YOUR LEGS AND LEAVE YOU PARALYSED!'

'EXACTLY!' SAID SQUIZZY. 'WITH ALL THE POLICE IN THE WORLD OUT OF ACTION, ME AND MY CRIMINAL MASTERMIND BUDDIES WILL BE ABLE TO COMMIT ALL THE CRIME WE WANT! WHAT DO YOU THINK, KID?'

'I THINK IT'S A TERRIBLE IDEA,' I SAID. 'WHY DON'T YOU USE YOUR SO-CALLED MASTER MINDS FOR GOOD INSTEAD OF EVIL?'

'FOR EXAMPLE,' I SAID, 'WITH ONLY A FRACTION OF THE BRAINPOWER IT TOOK TO CREATE THIS UNDERPANTS-SHRINKING MACHINE, YOU COULD HAVE FIGURED OUT A WAY TO:

'ELIMINATE WORLD HUNGER ...

'GET RID OF POVERTY ...

'ABOLISH WAR FOREVER ...

'AND EVEN REVERSE CLIMATE CHANGE!

'BUT, NO. THE BEST YOU BUNCH OF "GENIUSES" CAN COME UP WITH IS A MACHINE TO SHRINK UNDERPANTS!

'YOU OUGHT TO BE ASHAMED OF YOURSELVES!'

118 ⛵ BLAP!

SQUIZZY'S MURDEROUS EYES FLASHED RED.

HIS CRIMINAL MASTERMIND PALS JUST STARED AT ME.

I GULPED. ME AND MY BIG MOUTH! THIS TIME I'D GONE TOO FAR.

'YOU KNOW,' SAID SQUIZZY, 'IN ALL MY YEARS AS A CRIMINAL MASTERMIND, NOBODY HAS EVER SPOKEN TO ME OR MY CRIMINAL MASTERMIND PALS LIKE THAT.'

'I'M SORRY, SQUIZZY,' I SAID QUICKLY. 'I DON'T KNOW WHAT I'M SAYING. MY UNDIES ARE SO TIGHT THAT NO BLOOD IS GETTING TO MY HEAD. I MUST BE DELIRIOUS. PLUS I'VE GOT THIS AWFUL TOOTHACHE AND ——'

'NO NEED TO APOLOGISE!' SAID SQUIZZY. 'WHAT YOU SAID IS THE TRUTH, AND WE SURE AS HECK NEEDED TO HEAR IT.'

ALL OF HIS CRIMINAL MASTERMIND PALS NODDED. SOME EVEN HAD TEARS IN THEIR EYES.

'I MOVE THAT CRIME INC. CHANGE ITS NAME TO CARE INC ...' SAID SQUIZZY,

'AND, FURTHERMORE, THAT WE DISMANTLE THE UNDERPANTS SHRINKER ...

'AND DEVOTE OURSELVES TO MAKING THE WORLD A BETTER AND MORE CARING PLACE!

'ALL IN FAVOUR, RAISE YOUR HAND.'

EVERY SINGLE ONE OF THE CRIMINAL MASTERMINDS RAISED HIS HAND.

'HANG ON,' I SAID, 'BEFORE YOU DISMANTLE THE UNDERPANTS SHRINKER, DOES IT HAVE A REVERSE BUTTON?'

'WHY?' SAID SQUIZZY.

'BECAUSE I'M ABOUT TO DIE FROM THESE TOO-TIGHT UNDIES, THAT'S WHY,' I SAID.

'NO PROBLEMS,' SAID SQUIZZY. 'STAND ON THE SPOT MARKED X AND PREPARE FOR IMMEDIATE UNDERPANTS EXPANSION!'

I TOOK MY POSITION AND CLOSED MY EYES. ZAP! MY UNDIES WERE INSTANTLY EXPANDED.

ME IN LOTS OF BITS

'WOW!' I SAID. 'THEY'RE PERFECT! THANKS, SQUIZZY—YOU'VE MADE MY WORLD A BETTER PLACE ALREADY!'

I SAID GOODBYE TO ALL MY NEW FRIENDS AT CARE INC ...

CARE INC.

STAIRS

AND THEN RAN AS FAST AS I COULD TO SCHOOL ...

SIGN

SCHOOL ►

WELL, AS FAST AS YOU CAN RUN IN SUPER-STRETCHED, BAGGY UNDIES.

SNAIL ↑

REBUILD EEL

123

BUT AS I RAN I SAW WANTED POSTERS ON ALL OF THE LAMPPOSTS.

THE PERSON ON THE POSTER LOOKED LIKE ME. LOOKING CLOSER, I REALISED THAT WAS BECAUSE IT WAS ME!

THE POSTER READ: 'WANTED: ANDY "TIGHT UNDERPANTS" GRIFFITHS ...

'FOR INDECENT EXPOSURE, ATTEMPTED BURGLARY, JAILBREAK AND WEARING HIS UNDERPANTS MUCH TOO TIGHT.'

I KNEW I SHOULD TURN MYSELF IN, BUT I DIDN'T WANT TO BE LATER FOR SCHOOL THAN I ALREADY WAS, SO I KEPT RUNNING.

BUT I STUPIDLY STEPPED INTO A CUNNING BOOBY TRAP.

SUDDENLY I WAS HANGING UPSIDE DOWN FROM A ROPE, SURROUNDED BY POLICE ALL POKING ME WITH STICKS.

POKE   POKE

'WE KNOW WHO YOU ARE!' SAID THE POLICE. 'THOUGHT YOU COULD DISGUISE YOURSELF WITH A PAIR OF SUPER-STRETCHED, BAGGY UNDIES? WELL, THINK AGAIN!'

POKE

POKE

AFTER THEY FINISHED POKING AND TAUNTING ME, THEY CUT ME DOWN AND DRAGGED ME TO THE COURTHOUSE.

THE JUDGE SAID, 'YOU'RE IN BIG TROUBLE, YOUNG MAN! WHAT HAVE YOU GOT TO SAY FOR YOURSELF?'

'I CAN EXPLAIN,' I SAID. 'MAY I USE YOUR WHITEBOARD?'

THE JUDGE NODDED, AND GAVE ME A BLACK MARKER AND A POINTER. I TOLD HIM EVERYTHING THAT HAD HAPPENED ...

ABOUT THE TIGHT UNDIES ...

ABOUT THE JAILBREAK ...

AND ABOUT HOW I'D CONVINCED SQUIZZY AND HIS PALS TO GIVE UP CRIME IN FAVOUR OF CARE.

WHEN I FINISHED, THE JUDGE SMILED AND SAID TO THE COURT, 'THIS BOY IS NOT A CRIMINAL: HE IS A NATIONAL HERO!'

THEN HE SAID, 'AS A REWARD FOR YOUR GREAT WORK, I AM ORDERING A POLICE ESCORT TO TAKE YOU STRAIGHT TO SCHOOL!'

WE RACED THROUGH THE TOWN AT HIGH SPEED ...

STOPPING ONLY TO PICK UP MY TROUSERS, WHICH I'D TAKEN OFF EARLIER ON MY WAY TO SCHOOL.

I RAN UP THE STAIRS ...

THREW MY BAG ON THE HOOK ...

CAME IN HERE ... AND YOU SAID, 'YOU'RE LATE! AGAIN! WHAT'S YOUR EXCUSE TODAY?'

'So there you have it. That's my excuse. Nothing but the truth. The one-hundred-per-cent honest, cross-my-heart-hope-to-die-hope-to-stick-a-needle-in-my-eye truth about why I was late for school!'

I draw a deep breath. 'You do believe me, don't you, Mr Dobson?' I say.

But there's no response.

'Mr Dobson?'

I turn around.

Mr Dobson isn't there.

Neither are the other students.

The room is empty.

I look at the clock. School finished half an hour ago!

I was so busy explaining about the alarm clock and the tight undies and the teaspoon and the locked house and the nosy neighbour and the police and the jail and Squizzy and the jailbreak and Crime Inc. and the underpants-shrinking machine and the evil plan and all that stuff that I didn't even notice that the bell had gone.

Oh no! Now I'll be late home! My brilliant excuse for being late for school has made me late for my dentist's appointment!

Mum's going to KILL me ... or, at the very least, pull out my sore tooth with a pair of pliers!

Unless ...

unless ...

unless ... I come up with a really good excuse, that is ...

a really, REALLY good excuse.

(from page 48)
SPOT THE
DIFFERENCE
ANSWER:

(ALSO:
IS THIS THE
END FOR
MR SCRIBBLE
ANSWER
FROM PAGE 159.)
(AND PAGE 135.)

PAGE
97536

Why I love Choco-pops in fifty words or less

i love Choco-pops in fifty words or less because they are chocolaty, crunchy, cool, great, wonderful, amazing, exciting, lovely, yummy, etcetera, etcetera, etcetera, etcetera, etcetera, etcetera, etcetera, etcetera, etcetera, etcetera, etcetera, etcetera, etcetera, etcetera, etcetera, etcetera, etcetera, etcetera, etcetera,

etcetera, etcetera, etcetera, etcetera, etcetera, etcetera, etcetera, etcetera.
Yours truly,
Andy Griffiths

P.S. That's exactly fifty words, even counting the 'Yours truly, Andy Griffiths'.

P.P.S. I could have given you many other reasons why I love Choco-pops, but I was only allowed fifty words.

P.P.P.S. If you'd let me have more words I would have told you about how I love Choco-pops so much that I once ate five bowls of them, one after the other. I would have eaten a sixth bowl, too, except that I felt a bit sick and then, guess what? I really WAS sick! All over the kitchen floor. A big brown puddle of Choco-pops. Mum and Dad were really mad. Sooty was happy, though, because he dived in and started to eat them. Which just goes to show how great Choco-pops are—even dogs love them! In fact, Sooty probably likes them even more than I do, because as much

as I love them I wouldn't eat Choco-pops that somebody else had already eaten and then thrown up. Not even if you paid me a million dollars.

P.P.P.P.S. Not even a trillion dollars.

P.P.P.P.P.S. Not even a million trillion dollars.

P.P.P.P.P.P.S. Well, MAYBE for a million trillion dollars. I'm not stupid, you know.

P.P.P.P.P.P.P.S. Please don't tell anybody about me eating the five bowls of Choco-pops and throwing up, because it would be kind of embarrassing if that got around, plus I told Mum and Dad that I'd only eaten three bowls and they would be really mad if they found out it was five. They are always going on about how Choco-pops are not very healthy and how they are full of sugar and blah blah blah blah, but parents are always saying stuff like that. I think you'd probably sell a lot more

SHOCKING DRAWING (FROM PAGE 40) THIS PART WAS REMOVED ↓

THE REST IS ON PAGE 98.

133

Choco-pops if it wasn't for parents. You might like to look into this.

P.P.P.P.P.P.P.P.S. Then again, if it wasn't for parents you might not sell ANY because it's parents who have all the money, so maybe just ignore that last suggestion.

P.P.P.P.P.P.P.P.P.S. I especially wouldn't want it to get around that I spewed after eating five bowls of Choco-pops, because I don't think Lisa Mackney, the most beautiful girl in the world—or at our school, at least—would approve. She already thinks I'm a bit immature and I don't think it would help. And that would be a pity because things have been going really well since I built a time machine and used it to save the world from the giant slug that Danny had created for his science project. Well, when I say 'things have been going really well', I don't mean that things have been going THAT well. It's not like we're about to be married or anything. We're not even officially boyfriend and girlfriend. Or unofficially, either. In fact,

she hasn't even spoken to me since. But I think that secretly she still really likes me. I say 'secretly' because I heard from Suzie Smith that Lisa told her to tell me that she thinks I'm really immature and she DOESN'T like me and never will, but I think the only reason she said that is because she doesn't want anyone to know—not even me—and ESPECIALLY not Suzie, who would just go around and tell everyone, because you can't trust her to keep anything secret. Like the time when Danny put a love letter in her desk. The letter said, 'Dear Suzie, I love you. Do you love me? If you do, put a tick in the YES box. If you don't, put a cross in the NO box. From Danny. P.S. Don't tell anybody about this letter.' So what does Suzie do? She tells EVERYBODY about the letter. Poor Danny. He was SO embarrassed! Anyway, I know that's a bit off the point, but the point is that I don't think Lisa will be that impressed if she finds out about the Choco-pop incident, so please don't tell her. Or Suzie, because then, as I have explained, she will tell absolutely everybody.

MR SCRIBBLE SLEEPWALKS

ZAP!

IS THIS THE END FOR MR SCRIBBLE?

see page 130

135

VERY SHOCKING!

P.P.P.P.P.P.P.P.P.P.S. Another time I got sick was when my dad was reading Binky the Magic Kitten to me beside the fire one night. Jen, my older sister, was in the room as well and she was eating an orange. Dad asked her to get him an orange and she went to the kitchen and got one, but instead of giving it to Dad she stood at the door and rolled the orange across the floor—right into the fireplace and into the fire! Dad just looked at the orange burning in the fire and said, 'I wanted an orange, but not a hot one!' And, looking back at it, I don't know what was SO funny about that, but at the time it seemed like the funniest thing I had ever heard in my life and I laughed and laughed and laughed so much that I thought I would throw up, and then, guess what? I really DID throw up—all over Binky the Magic Kitten. Which wasn't very funny at all, because I really loved that book and we couldn't read it any more despite Dad's attempts to save it by smothering it in talcum powder and pegging it on the clothesline to dry out.

MR SCRIBBLE BUNGEE-JUMPING.

136

P.P.P.P.P.P.P.P.P.P.P.S. Obviously this is another story that I don't want getting back to Lisa or Suzie, so please keep this one to yourself—or yourselves—as well. I don't want Lisa thinking that I read books like Binky the Magic Kitten, because I don't. Well, not any more, anyway. Because that was when I was little. These days I only read books WITHOUT kittens in them.

P.P.P.P.P.P.P.P.P.P.P.P.S. Oh yeah, and horror comics.

P.P.P.P.P.P.P.P.P.P.P.P.P.S. The freakiest horror comic I ever read was called *Monsters of the Mind*. I'll never forget it. It was about this guy called John Restin who works for the US government. He has to deliver a briefcase containing a Top Secret report on the state of the Earth's defences against alien invasion to the President. But as John Restin is crossing the street, he sees a car heading straight for him! Somebody pushes him out of the way just in time, but he strikes his head on the road—which is better than being

(see, it's not the end for Mr Scribble.)

MR SCRIBBLE buys a horse.

I bought a horse.

THE END

PRESS

137

hit by a car, of course, except that when he comes to, he can't remember who he is, or who he's supposed to deliver the briefcase to. He looks inside the briefcase and discovers that it contains a master plan of the Earth's defences and realises that it must not be allowed to fall into the wrong hands. He stands up, picks up the briefcase and heads for a diner to try to collect his thoughts and remember who he is. He orders a cup of coffee, but instead of getting him coffee, the guy working behind the counter says, 'Time's up, John Restin; give us the briefcase!' and then he turns around and he's got this hideous alien face with huge fangs! John Restin freaks out. He doesn't know who 'John Restin' is or who the alien is—he just knows that he has to protect that briefcase. He runs and hides in a movie theatre. But when the film starts he sees the same hideous alien face on the screen—enormous this time—and it says, 'Time's up, John Restin; give us the briefcase!' Worried that he's going mad, John Restin runs from the theatre and straight to a psychiatrist. He's lying there

on the couch trying to figure out who he is, when the psychiatrist says, 'Time's up, John Restin; give us the briefcase!' Now John Restin is REALLY scared. He escapes out into the night. He gets into a cab and it takes off, but then the driver turns around and yep, you guessed it, he's an alien too. The cab is speeding across a bridge, but John Restin doesn't care. He just opens the door and jumps out, hitting the ground and breaking his leg. He drags himself along the side of the bridge. He sees a policeman up ahead in the fog, but when he gets closer he sees that it's not a policeman … it's another alien! The other aliens appear and close in around him. John Restin knows that they must not get the briefcase. But there's no escape. No way out … except for one. In that instant, John Restin chooses to sacrifice his own life for the welfare of the whole world. He throws himself—along with the briefcase—off the bridge. John Restin dies a hero's death, but as his lifeless body sinks down through the water, a strange thing happens. Out of his body comes—you'll never guess it—an

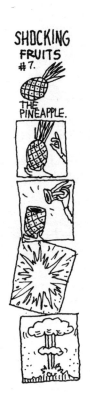

SHOCKING FRUITS #7.

THE PINEAPPLE.

139

alien with huge fangs! 'Now I remember,' says the alien. 'The briefcase! It must be delivered.' Clutching the briefcase it emerges from the river where the other aliens are waiting. 'We have waited a long time for you, brother!' says the alien in the policeman's uniform. 'Why did you resist us?' The alien who used to be John Restin says, 'It was the car accident, I hit my head and became dazed. I forgot that I was not truly an Earthman but one of you!' The other alien says, 'That car was no accident, brother. We arranged it to kill off your Earth-form so as to enable you to resume your normal being! But it doesn't matter now! With the secrets in this briefcase, conquering the world will be child's play! The Earthmen are doomed! Completely and utterly doomed!'

P.P.P.P.P.P.P.P.P.P.P.P.P.S. The reason I was so freaked out by this story was not just because the Earth is completely and utterly doomed, but because it really makes you wonder: how do you know that you're not absolutely wrong about who you think you

are? Or, to put it another way, how do you know that you really are the YOU that you think you are? Truly? How do you know that you're not really an alien disguised in the body of a human and that you've forgotten you're an alien and think that you are really a human being? Or have you ever wondered if you can be one hundred per cent sure that you're not just a character in a book, dreamed up by some writer with an overactive imagination? To tell you the truth, sometimes that's exactly how I feel. Some of the things that happen to me are so unbelievable that they HAVE to be made up. And sometimes I think that my friend Danny is SO dumb that he MUST be made up too. Nobody could be that dumb. But that's what I mean! How can you ever know for sure? How can I ever know for sure? Who am I? Who are you? Who are we? What are we? AAAGGGHHHH!

P.P.P.P.P.P.P.P.P.P.P.P.P.P.P.S. Sorry about that. I realise I shouldn't be asking you these questions. For all I know, 'you' don't even exist. Maybe they just back the

141

truck carrying all the entries up to a big bin and tip them in and then give the prize to the boss's children. That would explain why I've never actually won one of these 'Why I love something in fifty words or less' competitions, even though I've put about fifty thousand entries (or more!) in.

P.P.P.P.P.P.P.P.P.P.P.P.P.P.S. If you really DO exist, no offence intended. I just don't think it's fair that I NEVER win.

GIANT MUTANT KILLER CHOCO-POPS.

P.P.P.P.P.P.P.P.P.P.P.P.P.P.P.P.S. Speaking of horror stories, just imagine if there was a nuclear accident and somebody had left a packet of Choco-pops next to the reactor, and they all got irradiated and became giant mutant killer Choco-pops, and they're just rolling all over the place going 'Kill! Crush! Destroy!' (yeah, I know they don't have mouths, but imagine that these ones have little cracks where the words come out, which makes them even scarier, really), and the whole world is powerless against the giant mutant killer Choco-pops, maybe because some

BOO!

142

time earlier a Choco-pop disguised itself as an Earthman and stole the briefcase containing the state of the Earth's defences against invasions of giant mutant killer Choco-pops!!!

P.P.P.P.P.P.P.P.P.P.P.P.P.P.P.P.P.P.S. Ha-ha, the previous idea about giant mutant killer Choco-pops was just a joke. Please ignore it if you don't find it funny.

P.P.P.P.P.P.P.P.P.P.P.P.P.P.P.P.P.P.P.S. But if you DO find it funny, please feel free to award me extra points.

P.P.P.P.P.P.P.P.P.P.P.P.P.P.P.P.P.P.P.P.S. I think it would definitely make a really good TV ad. All those giant mutant killer Choco-pops rolling around killing and crushing and destroying, and nobody knows how to stop them until this boy genius comes along and says, 'Stand back everyone! I know just what to do!' And he grabs a cow, squeezes it and sprays milk all over the Choco-pops, making them go all soggy, and then the boy just sits down and eats them.

143

WIN A PRIZE
(CONTINUED FROM PAGE 30)

ANSWER TO QUESTION: A BALLOON.

OKAY, EVERYONE GOT THE FIRST QUESTION RIGHT. SO, NOW FOR A REALLY HARD QUESTION FOR ONE MILLION DOLLARS. TURN TO PAGE 347.
→ →

P.P.P.P.P.P.P.P.P.P.P.P.P.P.P.P.P.P.P.P.P.P. S. If you were looking for a boy genius to play the part, I am available and would LOVE to do it.

P.P.P.P.P.P.P.P.P.P.P.P.P.P.P.P.P.P.P.P.P. P.S. And I promise I wouldn't get sick, no matter how many bowls of Choco-pops you made me eat, because somebody throwing up Choco-pops everywhere would definitely not be the sort of image that would make parents rush out and buy Choco-pops for their children.

P.P.P.P.P.P.P.P.P.P.P.P.P.P.P.P.P.P.P.P.P. P.P.S. I'm sorry for bringing it up, really.

P.P.P.P.P.P.P.P.P.P.P.P.P.P.P.P.P.P.P.P.P.P. P.P.P.S. Get it? 'Bringing it up.' That was another joke. Please ignore it if you don't find it funny.

P.P.P.P.P.P.P.P.P.P.P.P.P.P.P.P.P.P.P.P.P.P. P.P.P.P.S. But if you DO find it funny, well, you know what to do.

ME NERVOUS WRECK!

P.P.P.P.P.P.P.P.P.P.P.P.P.P.P.P.P.P.P.P. P.P.P.P.P.S. Other people might say that they love Choco-pops, but I bet they don't love them as much as I do. I love them so much that, if I could, I would fill up a WHOLE room with Choco-pops and milk, and take my clothes off and dive right in and just swim around with my mouth open, sucking in Choco-pops and milk. That would be the perfect way to live. Especially if no matter how much you ate more kept appearing so that the room was always full of Choco-pops and milk. I mean, what more could you want? Well, maybe you'd want a toilet, because eventually, of course, you'd need to go and then it wouldn't be so great any more having to swim around sucking Choco-pops and milk and … I probably don't have to spell it out, do I? That would pretty much be the worst possible way to spend your life.

P.P.P.P.P.P.P.P.P.P.P.P.P.P.P.P.P.P.P.P.P. P.P.P.S. That last P.S. might sound a bit weird, but I just thought I'd mention it because I want you to understand how

much I love Choco-pops, and that I'm not just saying so to win a prize. Which raises another question: how do you check that these fifty words or less competition entries are true and not just made up by people so that they can win when they don't even care about Choco-pops the way I do? Do you have spies who go around checking to see that people are writing the truth? You know, sneaking into competition entrants' houses and reading their secret diaries and that sort of stuff?

P.P.P.P.P.P.P.P.P.P.P.P.P.P.P.P.P.P.P. P.P.P.P.P.P.P.S. Sometimes I sneak into my sister's room and read her diary, but I would advise you not to because it's drenched in perfume and girl germs and you'll probably DIE!!! Not that you'll need to read her diary, because she won't be entering the competition—she doesn't even LIKE Choco-pops! She prefers Fruit Crispies ... WHAT A SAD LOSER!!!!

P.P.P.P.P.P.P.P.P.P.P.P.P.P.P.P.P.P.P.P.P.
P.P.P.P.P.P.P.P.P.S. Please don't tell her I said that about reading her diary. She's sure to tell Mum and then Mum might be so angry that she won't buy me Choco-pops for the rest of the year as punishment. And that would only hurt you because I'm one of your best customers.

P.P.P.P.P.P.P.P.P.P.P.P.P.P.P.P.P.P.P.P.P.
P.P.P.P.P.P.P.P.P.S. It's a pity this is not a 'Who eats the most Choco-pops?' competition because I'd win that for sure.

P.P.P.P.P.P.P.P.P.P.P.P.P.P.P.P.P.P.P.P.P.
P.P.P.P.P.P.P.P.P.S. Well, that's pretty much it, now. Thanks for reading.

P.P.P.P.P.P.P.P.P.P.P.P.P.P.P.P.P.P.P.P.P.
P.P.P.P.P.P.P.P.P.S. Just one more thing—all these P.S.'s don't count as the words, do they, because if they do then I'm already 2675 words over the limit, which would pretty much disqualify me. So if they DO count, just pretend I didn't write them all and stick with the first fifty.

PARTS OF THE BODY YOU DON'T NEED #47: THE SPLEEN.

THE SPLEEN JUST SITS IN YOUR BODY SPLEENING. What use is that?

PLUCK IT OUT!!

THROW IT AWAY.

BURP!

P.P.P.P.P.P.P.P.P.P.P.P.P.P.P.P.P.P.P.P.P.P.
P.P.P.P.P.P.P.P.P.P.P.S. Please let me win.

P.P.P.P.P.P.P.P.P.P.P.P.P.P.P.P.P.P.P.P.P.P.
P.P.P.P.P.P.P.P.P.P.P.P.S. Oh yeah, and
if I win (please, please let me win), could
you just notify me by phone and not print
my name in the newspaper, because I
don't want Lisa to find out that I like
Choco-pops. I'd kind of rather she thought
that I ate something a little more healthy
and manly like Enduro-crunch.

P.P.P.P.P.P.P.P.P.P.P.P.P.P.P.P.P.P.P.P.P.P.
P.P.P.P.P.P.P.P.P.S. No offence to Choco-pops.

THE JUST
SHOCKING
STORY OF
SPLEEN
BOY
↓

ANGRY AND
ABANDONED
SPLEEN
BOY
ATTACKS...

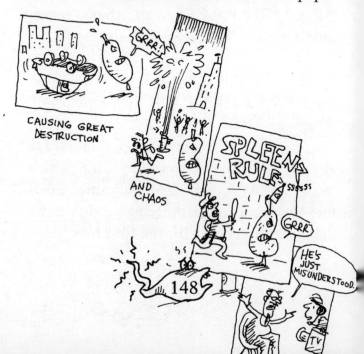

CAUSING GREAT
DESTRUCTION

AND
CHAOS

SPLEEN
RULE

sssss

GRRR

HE'S
JUST
MISUNDERSTOOD.

148

TV

Lemonade roulette

Danny and I are slumped over the kitchen table.

It's a hot day.

Too hot.

Hotter than the hottest day in the history of the universe.

In fact the word 'hot' doesn't even begin to capture just how hot this day is, no matter how many times you write it.

HOT. HOT. HOT.

Not even if you write it this big:

HOT. HOT. HOT.

And not even if you write it THIS big:

HOT. HOT. HOT.

This must be how it's going to feel in about four billion years when the Sun turns into a red giant and expands and engulfs the Earth and burns it up completely.

No, on second thoughts, even that day won't be as hot as this one.

'What have you got to drink?' croaks Danny.

'There's water in the fridge,' I say, rasping the words out of my cracked and parched throat.

'Is that all?' he says.

'I don't know,' I say, 'I'll check.'

I raise my head up off the table and sit up.

My head is spinning.

I stand up and walk slowly across the kitchen.

I open the refrigerator.

Cold air!

That feels better.

MUCH better.

I close my eyes and imagine that I'm standing in the snow.

On a really freezing day.

With no clothes on.

Mmmmmmmm ...

Usually Mum or Dad would come along and tell me to shut the door because I'm letting all the cold air out, but they're not here. They're playing golf with Mr and Mrs Bainbridge. And this IS an emergency.

If they were here, I bet they'd be standing in front of the refrigerator with the door open as well, imagining that they were standing in the snow on a really freezing day with no clothes on.

Well, actually, I hope that they wouldn't imagine that they didn't have any clothes on. I hate it when people imagine that they're naked when you're in the room with them.

Oh no! I'm imagining that I'm naked and DANNY's in the room!

I've got to put some imaginary clothes on my imaginary body.

Underpants.

Shorts.

T-shirt.

There. That's better.

MORE
SPLEEN
BOY.

GRRR.

RUNAWAY
SPLEEN
BOY
STEALS A
JUMBO
JET.

(For more
SPLEEN BOY
turn to Pg 163.)

(For less
SPLEEN BOY
try pg 457.)

BITE!
BITE!

151

I open my eyes and look for the water jug.

That's when I see them.

I don't believe it ... one, two, three, four, five, SIX!

Six cans of lemonade!

SIX!

SIX!

SIX!

They must be left over from our New Year's Eve party.

We're saved!

Six cans ought to be enough to get us through the next half hour at least.

'Andy?' says Danny. 'Is that six cans of lemonade I can see in your fridge or is it some sort of mirage?'

'You only have mirages in the desert,' I say. 'So these must be real.' I reach in and grab the ice-cold cans.

I take them back to the table with me.

Danny and I sit and stare at the cans in wonder.

I push one across to Danny and pick up one for me.

'Cheers!' I say, raising the can. I've got

my finger under the ring-pull and am about to open it when Danny stops me.

'Wait!' he says. 'Let's play lemonade roulette!'

'Lemonade roulette?' I say.

'It's like Russian roulette, where you have a gun that has six chambers but only one bullet,' he says. 'You spin the chamber wheel, put the gun to your head, pull the trigger and hope that the chamber with the bullet in it doesn't come up.'

SHOCKING GENETIC MIX-UPS #3.

MARSUPIAL MUFFLER MOUSE

'But why would you want to do that?' I say. 'You've got a one in six chance of being killed!'

'Yes,' says Danny. 'But you've got a five in six chance of NOT being killed.'

'Maybe,' I say. 'But if you don't play it at all you've got a nought in six chance of being killed.'

'That's not entirely true,' says Danny. 'Even if you DON'T play Russian roulette, anything could happen. You could get run over by a bus and then you'd be dead anyway. And you wouldn't even have had the fun of playing Russian roulette. But I'm not saying we play RUSSIAN roulette.

153

I'm saying we play LEMONADE roulette.'

'How do you play lemonade roulette?' I say.

'We shake one of the cans,' says Danny, 'and then we mix them up and we each have to choose one and open it right in front of our face.'

'What if it's the one that's been shaken up?' I say.

'Then you get covered in lemonade!' he chortles. 'Well?'

'It sounds really stupid and quite likely to backfire in some horribly unexpected way,' I say.

'So you're in?' says Danny.

'Of course!' I say.

We pick one of the cans and take turns to shake it.

Underarm shakes.

Overarm shakes.

Under-leg shakes.

Overhead shakes.

One-handed shakes.

Double-handed shakes.

No-handed shakes. Just kidding. There's no such thing.

We shake that can of lemonade more than any can of lemonade has ever been shaken before.

'All right,' I say, sweating from the effort. 'That should do it.'

'No,' says Danny, red-faced and puffing. 'Just one more shake.'

Danny takes the can and gives it a final, ultra-violent shake.

Then he puts it with the other five cans and shuffles them all around. I try to keep my eye on the shaken can, but Danny is too fast. All I can see is a blur of hands and cans. I can't keep track of the shaken one.

Finally he lines them up neatly on the table.

'Okay,' he says. 'We're ready.' He picks a can, holds it in front of his face, closes his eyes and pulls the ring tab.

Pfffssst.

Nothing!

He gives me a big grin and celebrates his victory with a long drink.

Then he puts the can down and wipes his mouth.

'Your turn,' he says.

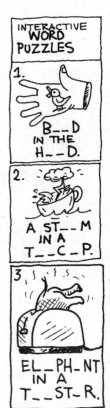

INTERACTIVE WORD PUZZLES

1. B _ _ D IN THE H _ _ D.

2. A ST _ _ M IN A T _ _ C _ P.

3. EL _ PH _ NT IN A T _ _ ST _ R.

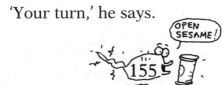

OPEN SESAME!

155

I take a deep breath.

I wish I'd gone first. Danny only had a one in six chance of getting blasted in lemonade. I've got one in five!

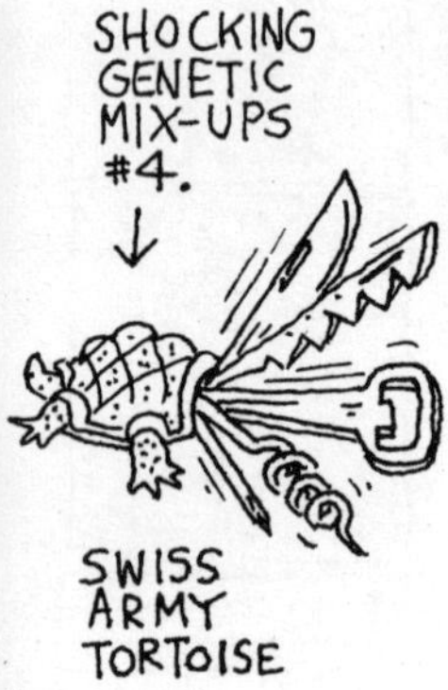
SHOCKING GENETIC MIX-UPS #4.
SWISS ARMY TORTOISE

I pick a can, bring it up in front of my face and pull the top.

Pfffssst.

Relief!

No fountain of lemonade!

I got away with it!

I take a long drink to celebrate.

Danny finishes his can, crumples it in his hand and lets it drop onto the table.

He's reaching for another one when the door opens. A blast of hot air rushes into the kitchen.

Dad walks in. His face is red and sweaty. Behind him is Mr Bainbridge, whose face is even redder and sweatier.

'The thing that most people don't realise about the game of golf,' says Mr Bainbridge, 'is that it's not about your swing—it's about your mind. I realised that many years ago, which I'm quite certain is the reason for my incredibly low handicap, not to mention my stunning

OPEN SEYMOUR!

performance out there on the course this morning.'

'Yes, sir,' says Dad as he stares open-mouthed at the cans of lemonade on the table.

'Mark my words, it's all in the mind,' says Mr Bainbridge, wiping his brow. 'In fact ...' He stops mid-sentence and stares at the cans as well.

'Just what the doctor ordered!' says Dad. 'Cold lemonade! That's very thoughtful of you, boys.'

'It is very thoughtful,' says Mr Bainbridge, approvingly. 'It's rare to see such thoughtfulness in young people today. They're all too wrapped up in their Xboxes and mobile phones and eepods to ...'

'You mean iPods,' says Danny.

'That's what I said!' says Mr Bainbridge, looking shocked. He's clearly not used to being corrected. Or interrupted.

EMOTIONAL
SWISS-ARMY
TORTOISE

'No, you didn't,' says Danny. 'You said "eepod", which sounds kind of silly.'

Oops. You don't talk like that to Mr Bainbridge. He fixes Danny with his 'that's the trouble with young people' stare.

OPEN
SLEDGE-
HAMMER!!

157

He draws a deep breath and is about to tell Danny a few more things about the trouble with young people when Dad cuts him off at the pass.

'Would you like a lemonade, Mr Bainbridge?' he says.

'Why … ah … yes,' says Mr Bainbridge.

Uh-oh.

One of those cans could be a lethal weapon. I can't afford to let it fall into the wrong hands. Dad's hands—and especially Mr Bainbridge's hands—are DEFINITELY the wrong hands.

Dad reaches for the cans.

'NO!' I yell, lurching forward onto the table and wrapping my arms around them.

'Andy!' says Dad, crossly. 'That is very rude. And very greedy.'

'That's the trouble with young people today,' says Mr Bainbridge. 'Very rude. And very greedy.'

'No, it's not that,' I say, thinking as fast as I can, which in this heat is not very fast at all. 'I just thought that you might prefer something else. Something a little more

SPROING!
CLICK!

158

suitable for adults. Beer, maybe … it's very cool and refreshing …'

Mr Bainbridge glares at me.

'Or so I've heard,' I add quickly, before he can give his opinions on young people drinking beer. (He's not in favour of it, in case you were wondering.)

'What a good idea, Andy,' says Dad, getting two cans of beer out of the fridge. He turns around and offers one to Mr Bainbridge.

Mr Bainbridge holds up his hand. 'No, thank you,' he says. 'I never drink alcohol during the day.'

'Me neither,' says Dad, turning back to put the cans in the fridge. 'Just joking.'

'Well, it wasn't very funny,' says Mr Bainbridge. 'I may have to review your position within our company if that's your idea of a joke.'

'But …' says Dad, his face turning from red to white in an instant, 'but …'

Mr Bainbridge slaps him on the back and lets out a loud guffaw. 'Relax!' he says. 'I was just joking!'

MR SCRIBBLE buys a nuclear ballistic missile
(THAT'S A MISSILE, AN EXPLODING ROCKETTY THING)

I bought a…

Is THIS THE END FOR MR SCRIBBLE? (see page 130)

KLUNK!

159

'Ah, yes,' says Dad. 'I knew that! Here,' he says, snatching two cans from my stash and handing one to Mr Bainbridge. 'Have a lemonade.'

'Thanks,' says Mr Bainbridge. 'Don't mind if I do.'

'Cheers!' says Dad, raising his can.

Mr Bainbridge raises his can in response. 'Cheers!' he says. 'Here's looking forward to a great year!'

A great year? With a can of lemonade blasted into his face? I am in such big trouble!

I look at Danny.

'What do we do?' I whisper.

He shrugs. 'Hope that Mr Bainbridge gets the shaken can,' he says. 'I don't like him very much.'

Danny's got no idea. I don't think he realises how serious this is.

Mr Bainbridge and Dad lower their cans.

They both put their fingers under the ring-pull at exactly the same time.

I can see the tips of their fingers ...
rising ...

up …

up …

up …

when suddenly the door opens again. Another blast of hot air fills the kitchen.

Dad and Mr Bainbridge both stop what they're doing and look up.

It's Mum.

Closely followed by Mrs Bainbridge.

Mum is looking hot, bothered and bored out of her brain. I don't blame her. Mrs Bainbridge is banging on about flower arranging.

SHOCKING GENETIC MIX-UPS #5.

ELECTRIC KETTLE PENGUINS

'The thing that most people don't realise about flower arranging,' says Mrs Bainbridge, 'is that it's not about arranging flowers—it's about arranging your mind. I realised that many years ago, which accounts for the high regard in which my flower arrangements are held, not to mention my stunning victory at the Garden Show this year.'

'Hello,' says Dad. 'We wondered where you'd got to!'

'We were just out in the garden,' says

REALLY DO NOT WANT THIS JOB ANYMORE.

161

Mum, sighing. 'Mrs Bainbridge was giving me some advice on our roses.'

'Well, we're just about to have some lemonade,' says Dad. 'Would you care to join us?'

'How about something stronger?' says Mum. 'I could really use a good stiff drink. What about you, Mrs Bainbridge?'

Mrs Bainbridge looks at Mr Bainbridge. Mr Bainbridge frowns.

'Oh no,' says Mrs Bainbridge, quickly, 'I never drink alcohol during the day.'

'Me neither,' says Mum, sighing even louder this time. 'I was only joking. Lemonade it is.'

'Lovely!' says Mrs Bainbridge. 'Did you know that flowers stay alive longer if you mix a little lemonade in their water?'

'No, I didn't,' says Mum. 'How fascinating. I'll be sure to try it.' She reaches across the table for the two remaining cans.

'NO!' I say, trying to snatch the cans away from her.

'Andy!' says Dad. 'I thought we just went through all this.'

'That's another thing about young

162

people today,' says Mr Bainbridge. 'They just don't listen …'

'Why can't I have the cans?' says Mum.

'Oh,' I say. 'Well, um, er, ah …'

'Yes?' she says.

I've got to think quick—
quick,
quick,
quick!

I've got it!

'How about I make you a nice cup of tea instead?' I say.

'Tea?' says Mrs Bainbridge. 'On a day like this? You've got to be joking!'

'That's the trouble with young people today,' says Mr Bainbridge. 'Tea, tea, tea … they NEVER stop drinking tea!'

'Isn't that OLD people?' says Danny. 'My grandma drinks about a thousand cups of tea a day.'

Mr Bainbridge just glares at him again.

'Thanks for your offer, Andy,' says Mum. 'It's very nice of you, but given how hot it is today we'd both prefer a cold can of lemonade. Could we have them, please?'

(FROM Pg 151.)
MORE SPLEEN BOY
GRRR!
SPLEEN BOY RAMS AN OCEAN LINER ONTO ULURU (Desert Monolith).
(Turn to Pg 168)

163

'Well, yes,' I say, 'but ...' I've got no idea what I'm going to say next. I can't think any more ... brain shrivelling up ... too hot ... All I know is that I can't let them get their hands on those cans!

'But what?' says Mum, becoming impatient.

'But you realise that they're full of sugar,' I say, without even knowing that I was going to say it. What a genius I am!

'What are you trying to imply, Andy?' says Mum.

'Nothing!' I say.

'Yes, you are,' says Mum. 'Are you trying to tell me that I'm fat?'

'No!' I say.

Mr Bainbridge sucks in his breath disapprovingly. 'If I'd talked to my mother like that, she would have come down on me like a tonne of bricks!'

'Was she fat too?' says Danny.

Oh no. That was DEFINITELY the wrong thing to say ... for so many reasons.

'I beg your pardon, young man?' says Mr Bainbridge.

'And what do you mean by "too", Danny?'

164

says Mum. 'Are you saying that I'm fat?'

I put my hand over Danny's mouth before he can reply and make things any worse.

Mum picks up the last two cans and gives one to Mrs Bainbridge.

'Hey,' I say, out of sheer desperation, 'who wants to play a game?'

'A game?' says Mr Bainbridge. 'Why yes, I love games! Most people think that games are a waste of time, but research shows that they can increase workplace productivity by up to eighty per cent. What do you have in mind?'

'Um,' I say. 'Last to open their can wins!'

'That's hardly fair, Andy,' says Dad. 'You and Danny have already opened your cans.'

'Oh yeah,' I say.

'We should make it the first one to open their can,' says Danny. 'Then I'd be the winner!'

I give up. I've really got to find myself a new best friend. A smart one.

'Congratulations, Danny,' says Mum.

A VERY
CONFUSED
MR SCRIBBLE.

165

COMING SOON!
- NEW -
PAGE NUMBER
HOST.

'Let's all have a drink to celebrate.'
They each raise their cans.
Time seems to slow down.
Their fingers slide under the ring-pulls.
Mum opens her can: pfffssst!
Mrs Bainbridge opens hers: pfffssst!
Dad opens his: pfffssst!
Mr Bainbridge opens his: Pfffsssssssss

SSSSSSSSSSSSSS
SSSSSSSS
SSSSSSS
SSSSSS
SSSSS
SSST!!!

ME PAGE NUMBER FROG.

166

A lemonade fountain!

I should have known all along it would be Mr Bainbridge's.

What I didn't know was just how much lemonade could come out of one can.

Mr Bainbridge is absolutely drenched.

Lemonade drips from his hair, his golf shirt, his nose.

It's even running off his ears.

Rolling down his arms.

Dripping off his fingers.

Forming puddles on the floor.

It's all over the front of his pants.

He's just blinking, spluttering, wiping his face clean.

Well, I guess that's it.

That's Dad's job gone.

That's my pocket money stopped.

Again.

But this time probably forever.

Dad glares at me. 'Did you have anything to do with this?'

'No,' I say.

But Dad continues glaring. Mum joins him.

Glare.

NOW PAGE NUMBER FROG TOASTER.

167

Glare.
Glare.

(FROM Pg. 163)
EVEN MORE SPLEEN BOY

GRR!

SPLEEN BOY, STILL ANGRY, PARKS HIS PINEAPPLE ON THE LEANING TOWER OF PISA.
(turn to page 211.)

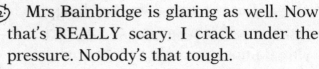

Mrs Bainbridge is glaring as well. Now that's REALLY scary. I crack under the pressure. Nobody's that tough.

'Maybe,' I say.

'Did you or did you not know that one of those cans was shaken?' says Dad. 'Yes or no?'

'Yes,' I say. 'But it wasn't my idea, it was ...'

I look around.

Danny's nowhere to be seen. No use blaming him. Nothing left for me to do but to pack my bags and check myself into the nearest adoption agency. Perhaps I'll be luckier the next time around.

I start to shuffle out of the room.

'Where do you think you're going, young man?' says Mr Bainbridge, finally recovering from the sugary blast.

I shrug. 'Not too sure,' I say, 'but I guess I'll find somewhere ... eventually ... till then I figure I can sleep in bus shelters ... under bridges ... live off whatever I can

STOP THIS

168

scrounge from rubbish bins ... maybe I'll jump a train heading north, pick fruit ... don't worry about me, I'll get by ...'

'Not so fast,' he says, approaching me with his hand outstretched and a broad grin on his face.

Huh?

Mr Bainbridge shakes my hand vigorously. 'I could use a young man like you,' he says. 'I thought your joke was very funny! Very, very funny!'

'You did?' I say.

Dad's glare turns to a frown, then to shock and then to relief as he realises that not only is Mr Bainbridge not angry, but he appears to be offering me a job!

APPENDIX GIRL SEETHES WITH JEALOUSY AT THE POPULARITY OF SPLEEN BOY.

'Yes!' says Mr Bainbridge, still dripping. 'It reminds me of a game we used to play as kids ... good old-fashioned fun. Now, let me see, what was it called ... so long ago, ah yes ... that's right ... lemonade roulette!'

'Really?' I say. 'You used to play lemonade roulette?'

'Oh yes,' says Mr Bainbridge. 'Some of the happiest days of my life were spent playing lemonade roulette! We didn't have

ME VEGETARIAN!

169

much, but we were happy … in fact, that's the trouble with young people today: they get too much …'

Mr Bainbridge is off again, but you know what?

For once I don't mind a bit.

I take a sip of lemonade.

Ahhh.

Cool and refreshing.

Nothing like a cold lemonade on a hot day.

170

SHOCKING BEDTIME TALES Pty Ltd

presents

The
Exploding
Butterfly
Story

Once upon a time there was nothing.

Nothing,

nothing,

nothing

and still more nothing.

Until, all of a sudden,

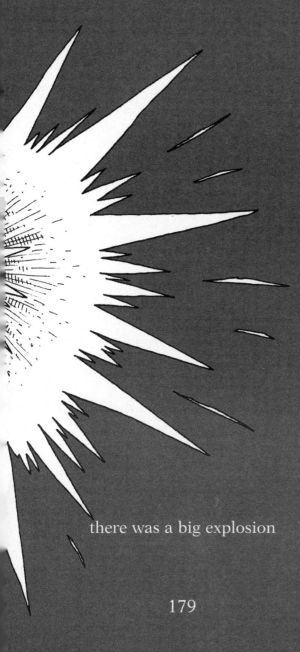

there was a big explosion

and out came the universe ...

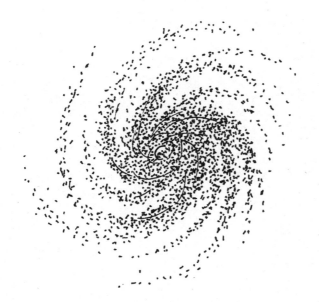

and the galaxy ...

and the Sun
and the planets

and the Moon
and the Earth

and every living creature on Earth,

185

including a very
pretty pink butterfly.

One day the
pretty pink butterfly was
fluttering in a sunny meadow
with lots of other
pretty pink
butterflies.

A beautiful little bluebird sang sweetly in the willow tree.

Fluffy white lambs frolicked
in the soft green grass.

Then,
    all of a sudden,

the pretty pink butterfly exploded.

Then another pretty pink
butterfly exploded.

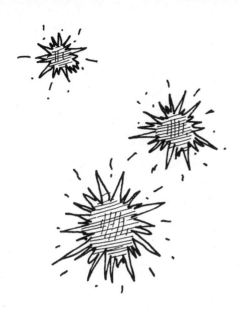

Then all the pretty pink
butterflies exploded.

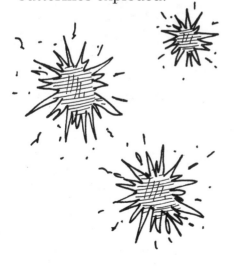

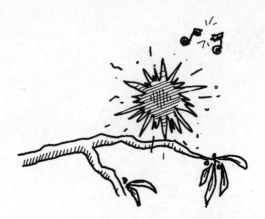

The bluebird exploded.

The willow tree exploded.

The fluffy white lambs stopped frolicking

and
exploded.

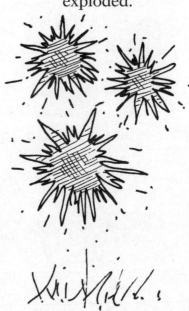

The soft
green grass
exploded.

The meadow
exploded.

A man walking past the
meadow exploded.

The man's wife exploded.

Every living creature on Earth
exploded.

Then the Earth exploded.

The Moon
and
the planets
and
the Sun exploded.

The galaxy exploded.

The universe exploded.

Then the explosion
exploded.

Then the explosion
of the explosion
exploded.

Then the explosion
of the explosion
of the explosion
exploded

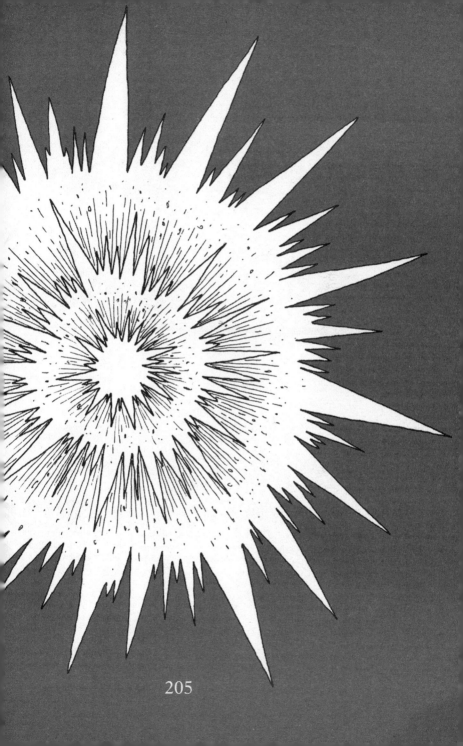

and that
was the
end because
all that was left
was nothing.

FUN WITH A MONSTER TRUCK

ANDY: Hey, Danny, I've been thinking, and you know what? I reckon we could have a lot of fun with a monster truck.

DANNY: Well, sure, but it depends on what sort of specifications you are talking about.

ANDY: Well, just the usual stuff. You know, something like a fibreglass pickup truck body with a 6.3 litre supercharged, alcohol-injected Chevy small block linked to a turbo 400 transmission with a manual reverse pattern valve body and a 4000 r.p.m. stall converter producing

ME MONSTER TRUCK EEL.

208

1500 wheel-standing horsepower, ZF axles with internal wet brakes and planetaries, eight nitrogen-charged custom-designed shocks on 66-inch Firestone Flotation tyres each weighing over half a tonne. That sort of thing.

DANNY: I can definitely see how we could have some fun with that.

ANDY: Yeah! We could drive around and if other cars got in our way we could just run over them and crush them to bits.

DANNY: You bet. And if any buildings got in our way, we could just drive right over the top and crush them as well.

ANDY: Great idea! And if we came to a zoo, well, we could just drive right in and crush all the buildings AND the animals! How cool would that be? Just imagine driving around the elephant enclosure crushing elephants underneath our 66-inch Goodyear terras!

DANNY: I don't know about that, Andy. I kind of like elephants.

ANDY: That's okay. We could crush hippos instead. They probably deserve it more than elephants anyway. Did you know that hippos kill more humans than any other animal in Africa? You don't want to mess with hippos. Not unless you've got a monster truck, that is.

DANNY: I'm not sure we should mess with hippos ... whether we've got a monster truck or not.

ANDY: What are you, a hippo lover or something?

DANNY: No, but hippos have really bad tempers. What if the hippos got hippo rage and got a monster truck and came after us?

ANDY: That's just stupid. Hippos can't drive.

DANNY: I know, but what if they could?

ANDY: Well, it's still stupid, because we would have already crushed all the hippos anyway.

DANNY: But what if some of the hippos

CRUSH CAR.

were out visiting the elephants and while they were there they saw what we were doing to the other hippos and they went and got their hippo monster truck and then came after us looking for revenge? We couldn't just drive over them, because they would have their own monster truck and the one thing that monster trucks definitely can't drive over and crush is other monster trucks.

ANDY: Well, that all depends. Is the hippos' monster truck as big as ours?

DANNY: Yes.

ANDY: Is it as powerful as ours?

DANNY: Yes.

ANDY: Does it have flame-throwing exhaust pipes?

DANNY: No.

ANDY: Well, that's easy, then. If they were chasing us I'd let them catch up, and then when they were really close I'd let

(from page 168.)

FAR TOO MUCH SPLEEN BOY

SPLEEN BOY CRASHES THE MOON INTO THE SYDNEY OPERA HOUSE.

HAS SPLEEN BOY FINALLY GONE TOO FAR? (turn to Pg 212)

CRUSH JUMBO!

211

the flames rip and incinerate the hippos and their stupid monster truck, and that would be the end of that.

DANNY: It might be the end of their monster truck, but what if the hippos had flame-retardant suits on?

ANDY: Now you're just being dumb. As if they would make flame-retardant suits to fit hippopotamuses! What would they even need them for?

(from Page 211)
HAS **SPLEEN BOY** finally GONE TOO FAR?

NO!

HEE. HEE.

DANNY: In case their swamp caught on fire … or somebody flamed their monster truck. How would I know? But that's beside the point. The point is, what if they had them on and they survived the flaming and now they were REALLY mad because not only did we just kill all their friends and families, but we just destroyed their monster truck as well?

ANDY: What do you think I'd do? I'd just reverse over the top of them and crush them like bugs.

CRUSH OPERA HOUSE.

212

DANNY: Yeah, but what if they were wearing specially designed monster-truck resistant suits?

ANDY: Now you're just creating problems for the sake of it! As if that's EVER going to happen!

DANNY: But it MIGHT happen. You can't be absolutely sure that it wouldn't. I know it's not likely, but it's possible. And if it did happen, what would you do? That's the question.

ANDY: No, the real question is—do you want to have fun in a monster truck with me or do you just want to go on and on about stupid hippos?

DANNY: Umm ...

ANDY: Take your time. Don't rush what could be the most important decision of your life.

DANNY: I want to have fun in a monster truck.

ANDY: Do you mean it?

DANNY: Of course!

ANDY: All right! You won't regret it, Danny. I promise. THIS IS GOING TO BE THE BEST DAY EVER!

ANDY GRIFFITHS & TERRY DENTON

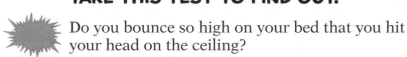

HELP! I'M TRAPPED IN MY BEST FRIEND'S NOSE AND 8 OTHER JUST CRAZY! STORIES

IS THIS THE RIGHT BOOK FOR YOU? TAKE THIS TEST TO FIND OUT.

Do you bounce so high on your bed that you hit your head on the ceiling?

Do you ever look in the mirror and see a maniac staring back at you?

Do you swing on the clothes line whenever you get the chance?

Do you sometimes get the urge to take all your clothes off and cover yourself in mud?

Do you often waste your time taking crazy tests like this one?

SCORE ONE POINT FOR EACH 'YES' ANSWER

3–5   You are completely crazy. You will love this book.

1–2   You are not completely crazy, but you are not far off it. You will love this book.

0   You are so crazy you don't even realize you're crazy. You will love this book.

A selected list of titles available from Macmillan Children's Books

The prices shown below are correct at the time of going to press. However, Macmillan Publishers reserves the right to show new retail prices on covers, which may differ from those previously advertised.

Andy Griffiths & Terry Denton

Help! I'm Being Chased By a Giant Slug		
(and 8 other Just Disgusting! stories)	978-0-330-50411-9	£4.99
Help! I'm Trapped In My Best Friend's Nose		
(and 8 other Just Crazy! stories)	978-0-330-50410-2	£4.99
What Bumosaur Is That?	978-0-330-44752-2	£4.99

Steve Hartley

Danny Baker Record Breaker:		
The World's Biggest Bogey	978-0-330-50916-9	£4.99
Danny Baker Record Breaker:		
The World's Awesomest Air-Barf	978-0-330-50917-6	£4.99

Paul Stewart & Chris Riddell

Blobheads	978-0-330-41353-8	£4.99
Blobheads Go Boing!	978-0-330-43181-1	£4.99

All Pan Macmillan titles can be ordered from our website, www.panmacmillan.com, or from your local bookshop and are also available by post from:

Bookpost, PO Box 29, Douglas, Isle of Man IM99 1BQ

Credit cards accepted. For details:
Telephone: 01624 677237
Fax: 01624 670923
Email: bookshop@enterprise.net
www.bookpost.co.uk

Free postage and packing in the United Kingdom